Never Ignore Monica

Jim Lively

TREATY OAK PUBLISHERS

PUBLISHER'S NOTE

**Printed and published in
the United States of America**

TREATY OAK PUBLISHERS

ISBN 978-1-959127-12-3

also by Jim Lively

ABERRANT BEHAVIOR
ARBITRARY AND CAPRICIOUS
CHOKING ON THE SPLINTERS
PUNITIVE DAMAGES
THE PUZZLE AESTHETIC
SURREAL ABSURDITY

Available inprint and digital on Amazon

DEDICATION

This novel was influenced in part by my experiences growing up in the Oak Cliff neighborhood of Dallas and attending twelve years of school in the Dallas Independent School District. It seemed only appropriate to dedicate it to all the friends and acquaintances I encountered during those twelve years.

I especially would like to signal out my classmates when I was in the sixth grade at Margaret B. Henderson Elementary School many years ago. That was without a doubt one of the happiest times of my life!

Chapter 1

November 12, 1960, was a cool crisp Saturday morning in Dallas, Texas. The neighborhood boys thought it was perfect weather for a game of sandlot football. The uneven vacant lot situated just behind Simon's house served as a football field in fall and a chigger-infested baseball field in summer.

The ten boys ranged in age from six to eleven. When they chose sides, Simon Steed, the youngest boy, was chosen last. The boys played non-stop for two hours and then decided that the next team to score would be declared the Oak Cliff Champions, named after the area in Dallas, where they resided.

Simon's team had the ball, but it was fourth down. They needed to score on this play or turn the ball over on downs.

The boys broke huddle and Simon jogged out to wide receiver on the left side of the line. He was dressed in blue jeans, a University of Texas T-shirt, and black Converse tennis shoes.

By instinct, Simon rubbed his blond burr haircut as he stared down the line of scrimmage, waiting for Gary Bayless, a husky boy four years older, to snap the football. Tommy Ross, a tall lanky boy who was five years ahead of Simon and the oldest of the ten boys, was the quarterback.

Steve, Simon's extroverted older brother, was a coordinated, athletic boy who played defense for the other team, covering Terry Sutherland, lined up at wide receiver on the right side. Terry was known for his speed and agility.

The other four boys on defense were poised, ready to rush the quarterback. Simon speculated the boys on defense knew Tommy was not going to throw the football in his direction, since no one even bothered to cover him.

Tommy clapped his hands twice, signaling the center and the O-line. After Gary snapped the football to Tommy, Simon jogged up the left side of the field around ten yards, whirled around, and froze to watch the play develop.

Tommy rolled to his right and appeared to be locked in on Terry, who was blanketed by Steve. Two of the boys on defense were closing in on Tommy when he suddenly rotated his head to face the opposite side. He planted his left foot and hurled the football across the field.

Simon's eyes widened when the football flew in his direction. He stretched out his hands as the ball drew near. It struck him firmly in the chest and bounced upward just out of his grasp. Simon watched as the football reversed its trajectory and fluttered toward the ground. He darted toward the football and was able to scoop it off the top of his tennis shoes.

A chill of adrenaline shot through him when he realized he had caught the football. He tucked it under his right arm, turned, and ran as fast as he could manage toward the bois-d'arc tree that marked the end zone.

A few yards from the end zone, Simon tripped on a bois-d'arc apple. The football fumbled out of his hands when he attempted to break his fall with his left hand. His brother Steve, trailing a few feet behind, snatched up the football and headed toward his team's goal line.

Simon remained on the ground, watching his brother celebrate scoring a touchdown with his teammates in the opposite end zone. Tears welled up as he trudged back up the field to where his teammates stood. All four boys wore frowns and were laser-focused on him.

"What a wimp!" Tommy yelled. "How could you possibly fumble the football?"

Simon whimpered, "I'm sorry."

Gary said, "We only let you play because we want Steve to play.

"That's right, Simon," Tommy said, "you're just weird."

Simon gasped, as if he'd been stung. He whirled around and ran through the field toward his house. He swung open the back door of his house and sprinted past his mother, Mary Ellen Steed, who stood at the kitchen sink washing dishes. When he reached the bedroom he shared with his brother, he jumped on his bed and cried.

I'm not weird, I'm smart! Why couldn't I have been the oldest son?

* * *

Monday morning, Mary Ellen pulled her Oldsmobile into the parking lot next to the building that housed the church's Sunday School classes and kindergarten where Simon attended.

His class was tasked this morning to color with crayons pre-drawn autumn leaves to be exhibited and adorn the walls of the small classroom. Along with his classmates, he took his time to select three leaves and then chose his crayons from the box in the center of the worktable.

His teacher, Miss Neely was a kind, gentle, fifty-year-old woman who always dressed in a simple dress with her silver hair pulled back in a bun. This morning, she gave the class thirty minutes to finish the task.

Simon colored as fast as he could, first with a red orange crayon, followed with an orange crayon, and then with a burnt orange crayon. Even years later, he could still remember the exact name of the crayons that he selected from the yellow orange and green containers that Miss Neely had carefully arranged on the worktables in front of them.

Precisely thirty minutes later, Miss Neely stood up from her desk and said, "Okay, everyone, it's time to set down your crayons."

Simon placed his crayons in front of him and inspected his leaves.

Looks pretty good. All my coloring is within the lines. I hope Miss Neely picks mine to put on the wall.

Miss Neely circled the room, stopping at every student's desk and peered over their shoulders. She stopped at his desk at last and then proceeded to the next desk.

"Dot, your leaves are perfect!" Miss Neely held up the leaves for everyone to see. They were magnificent with a rich bold coloring that resembled more of an oil painting than crayon colors.

How did she do that? We all had the same amount of time.

Miss Neely passed through the classroom again and selected about a dozen leaves from various students. When she reached Simon's desk, she paused. "Well, Simon, you stayed within the lines this time. You're improving."

Why did she single me out? I'm improving? Really, was that necessary?

All the students stared at him. The class was not accustomed to Miss Neely criticizing a student in front of the other students. Simon glanced at the perfect artist, Dot, who was smirking at him.

She thinks she's so perfect. Just wait, she will get

what's coming to her someday.

"All right, class," Miss Neely said, "it's time for our rest period. I want you to line up in single file and pick your blanket off the shelf."

Miss Neely referred to the class's down time as "rest period". Even as a six-year-old, Simon thought it was odd that the students were required to lie on a blanket upon a hard tile floor for thirty minutes without saying a word. Miss Neely did not tolerate any variance from this daily ritual.

As was Simon's custom, he selected a vacant spot near a corner of the room away from the rows of desks. Most students chose to lie down near their own desks. From his vantage point, he could watch the entire group, albeit from ground level.

As soon as the children were settled, Miss Neely said, "Dot, would you like to help me decorate the wall with your beautiful leaves?"

This was unchartered territory. Never had Miss Neely allowed a student to skip rest period.

Dot sprang to her feet. She wore a smug smile as she made her way through the prone bodies of her classmates over to Miss Neely's desk.

Why does Dot get to break the rules? I hate her!

Dot and Miss Neely spent twenty minutes arranging and attaching the chosen autumn leaves to the borders of the chalkboard. He was laser-focused on every movement Dot made.

Miss Neely said, "Thank you, Dot. Please return to your blanket for the remainder of the rest period."

Dot made eye contact with Simon and cracked what he sensed was an insincere smile. As she was nearing her blanket, her right foot snagged the corner of another student's blanket.

Simon smirked.

The blanket suddenly shifted, and Dot lost her balance and went tumbling into a row of desks. Her head struck the corner of one of the wooden desks and she crumbled to the ground.

Several students screamed and others burst out crying. Simon remained motionless and watched from his prone position.

From across the room, Miss Neely said, "Dot, are you okay?"

All the students except Simon were now on their feet, circling Dot's limp body.

Miss Neely rushed over to Dot. "Listen, everyone, take your seats now."

Simon remained lying on the floor.

Miss Neely shot a glance in Simon's direction. "Simon, why aren't you obeying me and taking your seat?"

He sat up, inch by inch."Because rest period isn't over."

"Well, if you're not going to take your seat, then go get the nurse. Hurry!"

Simon stood up and took care to fold his blanket and return it to the shelf.

"Hurry up, Simon, Dot's hurt bad!"

He walked out of the classroom and closed the

door behind him. The nurse's office was in the administrative building across a small courtyard. Simon exited the school and headed in that direction. It was a beautiful sunny crisp autumn day. A red cardinal landed right in front of him on top of a chain linked fence. He stopped in his tracks.

He paused a few seconds to stare at the bird.

I better keep moving. Otherwise, I'll get in trouble.

Simon ascended the steps that led to the front door of the administrative building. The inside of the 1930s building always had a musky moldy smell. Today was no exception. He ambled down the hallway to the end of the hall where the nurse's office was located and knocked on the heavy wooden door.

After a brief delay, the door swung open. Nurse Annabelle Coke was a plump woman who always wore a crisp white uniform. "Yes?"

"Miss Neely sent me to get you."

"Miss Neely? Why, what happened?"

"A girl fell down and hit her head."

The nurse rushed past Simon and hurried down the hallway. He followed at a distance. Upon exiting the administrative building, Simon watched the nurse open the door to the school.

He walked with serious deliberation back to the school. When Simon arrived at Miss Neely's classroom, the nurse and Miss Neely were kneeling next to Dot.

Chapter 2

May 17, 1966, Mrs. Westbrook opened the door to the classroom and hurried inside. She was carrying three white belts. A hush fell over the students.

"Okay, students, before we turn our attention to English, I have an announcement to make. Three boys from your fifth grade class have been selected to be school patrols for the remainder of the school year and all next year when you are in the sixth grade. A fourth boy is named as an alternative. He will be assigned as a patrol if something happens to one of the three.

"The criteria for selection is based upon academic standing and character. Each is given equal weight. Patrols must maintain excellent academic standing and good character during the entire school year. Principal Bowley will be joining us in a few minutes to make the formal presentation and swear in the new patrols. While we're waiting for Mr. Bowley, please pull out your English books and begin reading chapter three."

Simon fished out his English book from underneath his desk and flipped through pages.

I'm guaranteed to be named one of the three patrols. My grades are the highest in not only my class but every other fifth grade class. I wonder who else made the cut?

Before he could turn to chapter three, the door to the classroom opened and Mr. Bowley came inside. He was a short thin man, impeccably dressed in a gray suit that matched the color of his hair. "Mrs. Westbrook, may I address your class?"

"Of course. I have just informed them that you would be making the formal presentation naming the three patrols and alternate."

Mr. Bowley turned to face the class. "Ten patrols from the entire fifth grade class have been selected to be patrols of Margaret B. Henderson Elementary School. Three and a designate have been named from your class."

He pulled a sheet of paper from his coat pocket. "If I call your name, please come up to the front of the room to get your belt. You will then follow me down to my office where Vice Principal Epps and I will swear you in and discuss your roles and responsibilities."

Simon glanced around the room. Everyone's eyes were fixated on Mr. Bowley.

"The first patrol is Shawn Axtell."

I get that selection; Shawn's smart and a good athlete.

Shawn lumbered to the front of the class.

Mr. Bowley squinted his eyes as he stared down at the piece of paper. "The second patrol is Donald

Spelling."

Don? Is he kidding? Don's an idiot.

Don walked to the front of the class and stood next to Shawn. Don gave Shawn a playful nudge with his elbow.

Simon inched over in his seat so that he could get up when his name was called.

"The final patrol is Jimmy Powell."

Simon gritted his teeth as his face turned feverish. He glared as Mr. Bowley placed the sheet of paper back into his pocket and handed patrol belts to the three classmates.

"New patrols, please follow me." He then stopped short of the door. "I almost forgot." He pulled the piece of paper back out of his pocket. "The alternate is Simon Steed."

With an audible gasp, Simon ducked his head and refused to make eye contact with anyone.

Really? An alternate? I wish he just named anyone else. Why me? I should be the first name he announced.

Terri Drury was the brightest girl in the class and sat next to Simon. She looked over at him. and recoiled when she saw the expression on his face. "You look like you've just seen a ghost."

Simon sneered as he growled at her, "I didn't see a ghost. I see death."

Terri rolled her eyes. "You're weird, Simon!"

He said nothing else to her.

The next morning, Simon's mother pulled her Oldsmobile in front of the school. As she searched for a place to drop him off, Simon spotted Jimmy Powell standing by a water fountain near the entrance of the school. He was wearing his new white patrol belt, surrounded by several girls in the fifth and sixth grade classes.

These girls were always together. They were the elite clique in school. Most came from higher-income families and dressed in more expensive clothing than their peers could afford. Jimmy was right there among them.

Simon attempted to scuttle past them without being noticed.

Jimmy must have caught a glimpse of him. "Hey, Simon, Mr. Alternate Patrol."

The clique in unison turned their heads to face Simon. He thought they resembled some wild herd of deer hearing a twig snap.

A blond girl named JoAnne was their leader. "Don't talk to him," she said in a harsh tone. "He's strange."

Simon gave her his fiercest expression and continued past them into the school.

I wonder if the clique would be hanging out with me if I was named a patrol? Probably not. They think I'm strange just because I am smarter than they are.

The days went by and the excitement surrounding the naming of the patrols died down, but not for Simon. He was still incensed at not being named a patrol.

This must change. It's not fair. How can I make it fair?

On the night of July 13, 1966, an intruder butchered, raped, and murdered eight student nurses in a small Chicago apartment. The news of the mass murder shook Americans to the core. The entire nation was transfixed on who could have performed this heinous crime that cost these innocent young women their lives.

Mesmerized, Simon was one of them. His family was glued to the evening news on the family's black and white television each day following the crime. They listened and watched as Walter Cronkite announced, "Chicago authorities believe that the suspect was a loner and lifetime criminal named Richard Speck."

The prison photo of an acne-scarred thin man posing above a 'Dallas Sheriff's Department Inmate' sign flashed on the screen.

"He has not yet been apprehended. Authorities have learned, though, that before moving to the Chicago area, Speck had lived in a rundown area of east Dallas. It is possible he may be trying to get back to Dallas, where some of his relatives still live. If anyone has seen Speck or has any information regarding his whereabouts, please contact police immediately."

The part about 'possibly getting back to Dallas' shot shivers up Simon's spine.

What if he's in Dallas? What if he's here to kill more people?

"Simon and Steve," his mother said, "it's time for

you boys to go get ready for bed."

That was not the most comforting thing to see right before going to bed. Simon and Steve slept on bunk beds. When their parents first purchased the bunk beds, they let Steve, as the older brother, select which bed he preferred. He opted for the top bunk bed, leaving the bottom bunk to his younger brother.

Just because I'm younger.

Simon lay in bed most of the night, worrying about whether Richard Speck was going to break into their home. He reasoned that if he did, then Simon would be his first victim.

After all, he was the youngest in the family and stuck on the bottom bunk.

Chapter 3

It was recess on a hot September Thursday afternoon. All the boys in Simon's sixth grade class were dressed in white T-shirts and matching white gym shorts. The gymnasium, like the rest of the school, was not air conditioned.

Today's exercise was climbing the rolls of wood bars mounted from floor to ceiling on the two-story side of the gymnasium. Each boy was required to do five pullups on the top wooden rung before descending. The bars were wide enough to accommodate two boys at a time.

Simon waited in line behind Stuart Bradshaw, a stout, smart, blond boy. Stuart was Simon's only close friend. He was laid back and tolerated Simon's quirky nature.

Jimmy Powell stood behind Simon. Simon watched Stuart ascend the bars and struggle to do five pullups. After Stuart descended the bars and landed on the ground, he whispered, "Watch out! The bars are slippery."

Simon nodded. "Thanks."

He ascended the wall with no trouble. When Simon reached the top, he noticed a screw had come loose from one of the support braces that secured the pullup bar to the wall.

What do I do?

He grabbed the bar and did four quick pull ups. After his fifth pullup, Simon released the bar. The loose screw dislodged from the wall, dangling from the support. Simon descended to the bottom of the bars.

Should I tell Jimmy or Coach McNeil about the loose screw?

Jimmy scurried up the wall. He grabbed the bar and did four pullups. Midway through his fifth pullup, the support gave way and the bar, with Jimmy still gripping it, plunged downward.

His chin caught one of the other bars on the way down. He teetered for a split second before his body came crashing down face first to the wood basketball court below, still clutching the pullup bar. A pool of blood formed around his head and soaked the edges of his white T-shirt.

Coach McNeil ran over to Jimmy, bent down on one knee, and grabbed his wrist. "Damn!" he murmured.

A week after Jimmy's fall, he passed away. The cause of death was traumatic injury to the brain. Two weeks later, Simon was made a patrol. He stared down at the patrol belt that Jimmy Powell had worn.

I wonder if Richard Speck was a patrol?

Chapter 4

On the last day of his six-grade year, Simon's mother said, "Simon would you turn off the TV for a few minutes? Your dad and I have something we want to talk to you about."

Simon stood up, walked over to the television set, and turned it off. His dad and mother sat down on the sofa that faced the television set in their den. Simon returned to sit in a wooden rocking chair, the one he favored while watching television.

His dad said, "Son, we're moving across town. The neighborhood is changing here, and we feel like it's in our best interest to move to a safer part of town and get you into a better school."

"But I want to go to junior high school with my friends, and I like living here," he wailed. "We've been here my whole life. I won't have any friends if we move." He stifled a sob.

"We know, Simon," his mother said, "you have trouble making friends. Dear, it's just that now we must think about what's best for you and your brother."

"Does Steve know?"

His mother nodded. "Yes, we've already told

Steve. He's fine with the move."

Simon pouted. "I'm not! I don't want to move!"

"Simon, the decision has already been made," his dad said. "You'll see, it won't be that difficult."

Simon shook his head. "No, I'm not moving!" He jumped up without warning from the rocking chair and ran back to his room at the other end of the house.

During August of that year the Steed family packed up and moved from Wynnewood to southwest Oak Cliff.

Chapter 5

Mary Ellen Steed eased her Oldsmobile up to the side of William Hawley Atwell Junior High and shifted the car into park. Wearing a blank expression, Simon sat in the front passenger's seat, staring straight ahead.

"Simon, I know you're unhappy with your dad and me moving the family, but I promise you it'll be okay. It just takes a while to adjust to new things. I bet after a month or two, when you meet some new friends, you'll wonder why we didn't move earlier."

Simon opened the door and exited the car without saying a word to his mother. He trudged up to the side of the school building.

A man dressed in a dark suit, white shirt, and gray tie stood on the top of the steps that led to the door. As Simon drew near, the man grabbed Simon's arm, causing him to drop his notebook. It crashed to the ground. All his brand-new school supplies spilled out of the pockets of the notebook.

The man barked, "Do you know who I am?"

Simon trembled. "No sir."

"I am Vice Principal James Money and you, young man, are in trouble."

Simon's eyes widened. "I didn't do anything wrong."

James Money pointed at the ground. "Gather up your stuff. You're going straight to my office."

Simon was shaking but managed to retrieve all his school supplies and notebook. As soon as he stood back up, James Money opened the door and shoved Simon inside. He grabbed Simon by the upper part of his left arm and led him down the hallway.

A hush fell over the students who were mingling in the hall. They parted in the center as James Money led Simon to his office. Simon felt nauseous as he walked down the hall and thought he might faint at any moment.

All eyes were laser-focused on him. Whispers circulated among the students who were wondering what he had done.

James Money and Simon arrived at the front of the school where the administrative offices were located. A woman was seated behind her desk just inside the office.

James Money said, "Genny, please go get Miss Hill for me. I want to confirm that this boy is the one who broke her window."

To Simon, he gestured with his left hand toward a closed wooden door with the words 'Vice Principal' emblazoned on a bronze plate mounted in the center. "Go on in my office and sit down."

Simon did as he was instructed. He sat down on an uncomfortable wooden bench just to the right of the door in front of a large wooden desk. The door closed behind him.

After a few seconds, his eyes darted around the office. The desk was covered with various papers and a framed portrait of a woman setting on the side. Simon suspected that the woman was the Vice Principal's wife. Two college degrees were framed on the wall to the left of the desk and a picture of a mountain covered with snow was on the wall to the right.

Under the picture of the mountain was a large wooden paddle hanging on a hook. A chill shot down his spine.

Oh my God, I wonder if he's going to whip me with that paddle.

Simon took several deep breaths, trying to calm his nerves. Voices came from outside the door, but he could not make out any words. A muffled bell rang in the adjoining hallway outside the administrative office. Simon guessed it was the tardy bell that rang precisely ten minutes after the initial bell sounded, announcing the start of first period.

He swallowed hard when the door to the office opened. James Money and a young brunette teacher dressed in a simple gray dress with black flats entered the room.

James Money said, "Is this the one?"

She studied Simon' face for several seconds. "No, the boy who broke my window was older than this one."

James Money sighed. "Are you positive, Miss Hill?"

The woman nodded, "Yes, I'm positive."

"Okay, we'll keep looking. Thank you for coming to the office."

She cracked a half smile. "Of course, Mr. Money."

As she walked out of the office, Simon eyes were fixated on James Money, whose gaze seemed glued to Miss Hill as she exited the office.

James Money whispered, "Wow, what an ass."

James Money closed the door behind her and walked over and flopped down into the chair behind his desk. He shuffled a stack of papers in front of him.

Simon wondered if the vice principal had forgotten that he was in the office.

After a few minutes, James Money looked over his desk at Simon. "What's your name?" he snarled.

Simon cleared his throat. "Simon Steed."

The vice principal sneered at him. "Where are you supposed to be for first period?"

"Mrs. Carnes' English class."

James Money leaned back in his chair. "I know what class Mrs. Carnes teaches."

Simon ducked his head to stare at his shoes. "Yes sir."

James Money shot to his feet. "Let's go. I'll escort you there."

Simon followed the vice principal on a circuitous route on the first floor which passed by Miss Hill's classroom. The vice principal hesitated just a bit at the open door and smiled in the direction of Miss Hill, who stood at the front of the room, facing the chalkboard.

He tugged Simon's right arm. "Let's go."

They ascended a flight of stairs to the second floor and walked down the hall until they reached Room 211 and paused at the doorway. Mrs. Carnes was calling roll but stopped when she spotted them.

The vice principal said, "Sorry to interrupt you, Mrs. Carnes. Simon here seems to have lost his way to your classroom this morning."

He's making it sound like it was my fault that I was late to class. What a jerk!

She grimaced. "Thank you, Mr. Money."

He waved over his shoulder and exited the classroom.

I bet he can't wait to walk by Miss Hill's room again so he can stare at her.

Simon stood in front of the class. As he scanned the room, he noticed all the students' eyes were fastened on him.

Mrs. Carnes said, "Simon, what's your last name?"

"Steed."

Mrs. Carnes studied a piece of paper on her desk for a few seconds. "Okay, I see your name." She pointed to the left side of the room. "You can sit in the next to the last seat on the second row."

Simon shuffled over to the second row. A husky

boy, whose sneer seemed to grow the closer Simon drew near, occupied the last seat in his row. Simon plopped down in his chair and slid his notebook under his desk. Something or someone shoved his chair from behind. He glanced over his shoulder. The boy behind him mouthed the word 'loser'.

The rest of Simon's first day of school did not fare any better. He knew no one in the entire school.

A girl in his third period class asked him what he did to get in trouble with Vice Principal Money. A boy in his six-period class crashed a paper airplane into his head from across the room.

His math teacher, Mr. Easter, turned around from writing on the chalkboard to catch Simon picking up the airplane from the floor. Simon was required to stay fifteen minutes after school for disturbing the class.

As he sat in the empty classroom, he felt lonely and scared. Simon was never so glad in his life to spot his mother's Oldsmobile parked next to the curb when he exited the school.

When he slid into the front passenger seat, his mother said, "Why were you so late leaving school today?"

Simon sneered. "No reason."

She sighed, "Okay then, how was your first day in junior high?"

He pursed his lips. "Fine."

* * *

At 8:00 p.m. that evening, Mr. and Mrs. Steed were entertaining several couples in the living room. Simon and his older brother bickered over what to watch until they found the classic 1931 movie, *Dracula*, starring Bela Lugosi. The brothers' eyes were glued to the black-and-white television in the den.

Simon had watched several horror movies ranging from *Psycho* to *Frankenstein*. But there was something about this movie that resonated with him. He was enthralled with the dominance Dracula possessed to control the minds of his various victims. They were powerless to resist his mental manipulation of their actions.

He stayed awake for several hours in bed that night, not because he was afraid, but rather pondering whether he could somehow mimic Dracula's powers.

Could I also be a Prince of Darkness?

Chapter 6

Somehow Simon managed to survive his first month of junior high. His teachers became cognizant that he was quite intelligent, although very introverted and aloof. Several of them praised his academic achievements aloud in class in the effort to bring him out of his shell.

Although he was a loner, Simon did make a few friends. He was not close to anyone but at least let his guard down on a few occasions.

Simon had only encountered Vice Principal Money a few times in the hallway when changing classes. As far as Simon could observe, the vice principal did not seem to recognize him or treat him differently than any other student.

The weekly pep rally during football season took place every Friday afternoon. He did not much like any of the football players because most of them struck him as arrogant buffoons.

The only reason he attended the pep rally was to avoid sitting alone in a classroom. That would draw attention from the other students who would presume that he was being disciplined for some violation of school rules.

Simon seated himself in the second row of the auditorium where he had an unobstructed view of the entire stage. Everyone stood when the school band played the Atwell alma mater.

Twenty minutes into the assembly, Vice Principal Money strolled out to the center of the stage. He wore his usual severe expression. When the students spotted him, a hush came over the crowd.

"Some mischievous boys, who think they are really being cute, spray-painted several curse words inside the boy's restroom on the second floor. Actions have consequences. Because of this despicable act, I am cancelling the remainder of the assembly. Everyone is to return to your sixth-period class right now."

The adolescent crowd let out some muted boos. As Simon waited to exit the second row, the vice principal stood on the floor in front of the stage, surveying the auditorium.

Two football players, dressed in blue jeans and their matching letter sweaters, were attempting to lift and move a heavy wooden podium perched on the edge of the stage. It was often used as a prop by the cheerleaders when they performed a skit poking fun at the week's opposing team.

A cable rested on the stage, a few feet behind one of the boys. Simon froze in his tracks as he watched the boys draw near the cable.

Do it! Trip on it!

The boy backing up noticed the cable at the last second and stepped over it. Simon frowned. The boys continued easing the podium across the stage.

Simon stayed laser-focused on the two football players as they proceeded to finish their task. The boy edging forward reached the cable. His foot wedged in between the cable and the stage, and he lost his balance and fell. He never released the podium and plunged along with it.

Both the football player and podium struck Vice Principal Money squarely in the head and his legs crumbled beneath him. The crash resonated throughout the auditorium.

Several of the remaining students in the auditorium let out a collective scream when they realized what had happened. Simon smiled and then scooted down the aisle toward the rear door. He paused before exiting and stole a glance at the mayhem near the stage.

Bela would be proud!

Chapter 7

The fall of 1972 was warmer than usual in southwest Oak Cliff. Simon was scheduled to start his senior year at David W. Carter High School. His high school experience turned out to be a disaster for not only Simon, but also for hundreds of his Black classmates.

The Federal District Judge for the Northern District of Texas ordered the immediate integration of the Dallas Independent School District. Like most similarly situated school districts, Dallas ISD sought to comply with the order through mandatory busing. Instead of busing white students to predominantly Black schools and vice versa, Dallas chose just to bus Black students.

To no one's surprise, the Black communities did not receive this plan well. The Black students resented having to leave their current schools to attend a school far from home.

To exacerbate matters, the school district did not possess an adequate number of buses to implement this ill-conceived plan. Carter High School was one of the mostly white schools targeted as the new home for hundreds of Black students who currently attended South Oak Cliff High School in their own neighborhood.

The relocated students who were not able to ride on school buses were told to take Dallas city buses and request vouchers from the school district to cover the costs. The problem with this approach is that the Dallas city buses did not always have routes to accommodate this initiative.

Simon arrived early at school in the used 1966 Pontiac Lemans that his dad purchased for him the prior year. As he entered the school building from the student parking lot, he recognized a lot of familiar faces. Since the seventh grade, in his mind he had placed every student he encountered into one of three categories: Tolerable, Intolerable, and Friend.

The category of Intolerable students was occupied by most of the student body, followed by Tolerable. The Friend category contained less than a dozen students. Among the Intolerable students was a subset of around two dozen or so boorish boys whose only accomplishment was to be teammates on a losing football team.

Simon referred to them as the 'Jocks'. He speculated that high school football would be the apex of their lives. As such, they were determined to enjoy life to its fullest, which included bullying everyone they deemed undesirable. One of the boys in this group, Bobby Hixson, spotted Simon when he rounded the corner of the hall.

Bobby said, "Look who crawled in for his final

year of high school, Mr. Smart Weirdo."

Despite the eighty-degree plus temperature, all the boys in the group were dressed in identical powder-blue letter jackets, blue jeans, and tennis shoes. They all turned to face Simon, who attempted to skirt by them without incident.

Bobby stuck his foot out to trip Simon. Instead, Simon jumped over Bobby's outstretched foot and cleared it with ease.

The quarterback on the team, Jimmy Grimes, said, "Would you look at Simon? He's as nimble as a fairy."

Bobby chimed in. "If he's as nimble as a fairy, then he must *be* a fairy."

The whole group cackled in delight at that comment. Simon hurried down the hall without saying a word. His cheeks were flushed with anger.

I predict one day soon!

As Simon continued down the hallway, he approached the front of the school. The two doors to the school were propped open. The school's principal, Harold Lichenwald, stood to the side at the entrance.

Simon caught a glimpse through the open doors of several yellow school buses parked in the driveway. He froze in his steps and watched as the new students from south Oak Cliff filed into the hallway for the first time. Their eyes darted around, surveying the inside of their new high school.

Simon could sense their discomfort. He could only imagine how the Jocks and other Intolerable students would react when they encountered these new students.

* * *

In fifth period, Simon sat in the last chair of row three in his American History class. Bobby Hixson sat in the middle of row four, next to the wall. Sitting in front of him was Walter Lee, a Black student. He was the only Black student in the entire class.

Next to Bobby sat Mark Brigham. Both boys were decked out in their matching powder blue-and-white letter jackets. Five minutes before the end of class, Bobby leaned across the aisle and whispered something to Mark. He smiled and nodded.

Simon kept his eyes fixated on Bobby for the remainder of the period. As soon as the bell rang, Bobby sprang to his feet and hustled up the aisle. As he walked past Walter, he slammed his notebook in the back of his head. Walter's head jerked forward from the impact.

Bobby said, "Sorry, I guess I didn't see you there. Which makes sense, since you aren't supposed to be in my school anyway."

Walter rubbed the back of his head but did not respond. Simon's stomach lurched and twisted. He was used to being on the receiving end of the bullying.

Very soon, Hixson!

* * *

Simon sat in his sixth period Business Law class. His teacher, David Andrews, was absent, which meant the class had turned into a study hall. The substitute teacher did nothing but check the roll. Simon found this class to be more than interesting. He did not need a teacher for this course or any other one for that matter. He read the entire textbook after the first day of class and could tell ever since that the teacher was winging it.

To the annoyance of Mr. Andrews, Simon often corrected him when the teacher misstated anything from what was written in the book. It did not matter how trivial the error was on the part of the teacher.

Today, Simon was focused on something other than business law. He was still seething over what he had witnessed in his history class. Simon surmised that Bobby Hixson and the rest of the Jocks were most likely practicing on the football field just behind the school.

He was deliberating whether this was the right time, when the bell rang. He jerked up from his seat and grabbed his books from underneath his desk. Simon had been in a trance-like state of mind for most of the period.

The hallways of the school were packed with students hurrying to escape the confines of the school for the day. Simon sat in his Pontiac in the parking lot, staring at the football field. The team was separated into different groups running drills.

He glanced over at Bobby Hixson's brand-new Chevrolet Camaro, accessorized with all the bells and whistles, down to the shiny wire hubcaps. All of a sudden, Simon had an epiphany. He recalled over-hearing a conversation last year in one of his classes between two of the Jocks concerning a Friday night ritual during football season.

After each game, several teammates would meet in the student parking lot to down a few beers that had been acquired by illicit means, either to celebrate the victory or commiserate a loss. With the makeup of the current team, it was often the latter. Simon surmised that Bobby Hixson was the ringleader and would surely be a participant.

Simon cracked a smile.

Friday night might be a perfect time!

Chapter 8

Saturday morning, Simon lay in bed, wondering what may have happened the night before. After breakfast, he grabbed the keys to the Pontiac off the top of his dresser and informed his mother that he needed to get some gas for his car.

She smiled and nodded but did not look up from the newspaper. His dad had left early that morning for his usual tee time at the Oak Cliff Country Club.

Simon turned left on Camp Wisdom Road but did not proceed straight ahead to the nearest service station a few blocks down the street. Instead, he took an immediate right on Indian Ridge Trail, which wound through the neighborhood before reaching the practice field behind Carter High School.

When Simon arrived at the practice field, he took a left on Algebra Drive and another right on McKissick Lane, which ran along the east side of the campus.

He eased the Pontiac south down the street where the student parking lot was located near the school building. A barbed wire fence bordering the east side of McKissick Road separated rural southwest Oak Cliff from the urban development to the immediate west.

When he was within a hundred feet of the student parking lot, Simon slammed on the breaks.

The barbed wire fence parallel to the Pontiac had been breached to a severe degree. One of the posts was uprooted and lying on top of a pile of broken glass near the curb. The remnants of a yellow crime scene tape fluttered in the morning breeze attached to the post nearest the breach.

After pulling over to park, he exited his car and strolled to where the breach had occurred. Rubber skid marks streaked the street. Simon examined the prone post and found traces of dried blood on one end of the post. The barbed wire which connected the post to the next post to the south was severed.

He rubbed his chin, taking in the whole scene.

Simon glanced around to see if anyone was around. Satisfied that he was alone, he went over and tore off the remnants of the crime scene tape and returned to his Pontiac. Simon sat in his car for a few seconds, pondering what he had just witnessed. He did not have a clear vision of what had transpired.

Bobby Hixson must have wrecked his car! I wonder if that was his blood?

When he entered his house, Mary Ellen said, "Did you get your car filled up?"

Simon gave her a blank stare. "No, I forgot."

She shook her head. "Where did you go then?"

He shrugged. "I just drove around for a while. Nowhere in particular."

Mary Ellen frowned. "Simon, I worry about you sometimes."

Simon did not respond and walked past his mother back to his room. He pulled the crime scene tape out of his pocket and pinned it to the bulletin board above his chest of drawers.

Simon lay down on his bed. Although he had coveted the top bunk bed, he opted to remain on the lower bed after his brother went off to college.

A car crash I expected, but a crime scene?

Chapter 9

Monday morning at 7:45 a.m., Simon turned the corner onto McKissick Lane. As he drove a few feet down the street, he slowed the Pontiac to a crawl. A small group of students huddled around the breach in the fence.

Simon maneuvered past the group and parked in the student parking lot. Upon entering the school building, he found the hallway was full of students but unusually quiet. Several students spoke in hushed tones. Simon speculated they were discussing what caused the breach in the fence.

He located his desk in his first period classroom and sat staring straight ahead as the room filled up with students one-by-one. As was customary for Monday mornings, the class did not begin until after the principal, Harold Lichenwald, addressed the student body over the public address system.

Simon wondered if the principal would mention the breach in the fence which bordered McKissick Lane. A few minutes passed before a chime rang on the public address system.

Principal Lichenwald cleared his throat. "Good morning, students. Unfortunately, I have some tragic news to report to you this morning."

He paused and then sighed into the micro-phone. "You may have noticed the damaged fence on McKissick Lane. It was the scene of a horrific traffic accident last Friday night. Bobby Hixson was driving with Jimmy Grimes in the front passenger seat. I don't know all the specifics, but the car somehow struck the fence, causing one of the posts to uproot and pierce the front windshield of the car."

The principal exhaled. "Jimmy Grimes was pronounced dead at the scene and Bobby sustained some injuries requiring hospitalization. He's being treated at Methodist Hospital. I know this is terrible news for all of us who love these two fine young men. Please keep them in your thoughts and prayers. Due to the circumstances, I am going to suspend all other announcements this morning. Thank you."

A chime sounded over the system signifying the end of the announcement.

Simon scratched his head. He was shaking.

I didn't see Jimmy's death!

* * *

On Tuesday, news got around that Bobby Hixon had been charged with 'Intoxication Manslaughter' for the death of Jimmy Grimes. While Simon did not like Jimmy in the slightest, he did not wish him death. He was still perplexed that he could not envision the death.

Well, at least Bobby will pay a dear price for his behavior!

Simon gasped when he spotted Bobby eating lunch with his fellow Jocks. He later learned that, after Bobby was arraigned, District Court Judge Barrett was lenient in setting bail for Bobby. He took into consideration Bobby's stellar character.

During the arraignment proceedings, it was revealed that Bobby was a good student, a captain of the football team, and president of the Carter High School chapter of the Young Athletes for Christ.

Over the objection of the district attorney, Judge Barrett released Bobby on his personal recognizance. Bobby's family did not have to pay a penny to spring him. He was free to attend school and do his usual activities until trial as long as he stayed out of trouble.

Instead of being shunned by the student body and faculty for killing his friend, Bobby seemed more popular than ever. He became an even bigger celebrity at school.

During lunch, Simon and his friend Mike Hayes were seated at a table next to the wall by themselves. Simon spotted Bobby saying something to two Jocks and motioning with his head in Simon and Mike's direction.

Simon said, "Trouble's coming."

Mike whispered, "Can you believe this jerk? He kills his friend and then acts like nothing's wrong."

The Jocks approached Simon and Mike's table and

stood right behind Mike. Bobby reached down and picked up a cookie off Mike's plate. He said, "Sugar is bad for losers," and plopped it into his mouth.

Simon could not hold his tongue. "Being a loser is still superior to being a killer."

Bobby's face instantly turned crimson. "What did you say, freak?"

Simon spotted the vice principal approaching from behind the Jocks. "All I said was, I'm sorry about what happen to Jimmy."

Bobby leaned across the table and glared at Simon.

Vice Principal Davis said, "What's going on here?"

Bobby's eyes widened and he straightened back up.

Simon said, "Mike and I were expressing our sorrow at what happened Friday night to Bobby."

Bobby's nostrils flared and he clinched his fists at his side. "Simon, you—"

Vice Principal Davis placed his hand on Bobby's shoulder. "Bobby, don't risk it. Remember, you need to keep your nose clean until your trial."

Bobby let out a heavy sigh as he and the Jocks ambled away.

Chapter 10

After the six-period bell sounded, Simon made his way to the student parking lot. As he exited the building, he shot a glance over his shoulder.

Bobby Hixson's hulking figure was decked out in full pads in his practice uniform, leaning against the fence that separated the practice field from the parking lot. Three members of the drill team, named the 'Calicos', surrounded him. They were all decked out in bell bottom blue jeans and matching red coats with Calicos emblazoned on the back.

Simon surmised that the players were taking a breather from practicing and that Bobby was using it to flaunt his celebratory status. His car was parked a few feet from where Bobby and the girls stood. None of the group seemed to notice Simon as he strolled by and climbed into his Pontiac.

He rolled down the window on the driver's side, which was nearest the group, and smiled before cranking up the Pontiac. He recalled that he had a cassette tape in his car of John Lennon's recently released album, *Imagine.*

A few days earlier, he had overheard a conversation between Bobby and one of the school cheerleaders where he stated that he was furious that John Lennon had dared imagine that there is no heaven, which is expressed in the title song, "Imagine".

Simon cranked up the volume to the highest level. His friend, Mark Bowers, had helped him install the tape deck and speakers into the old Pontiac a few weeks ago. It gave the 1966 Pontiac a modern 1970s sound.

Simon rolled down his window, started the car, and then sat idling while he rewound the tape to the very beginning. The first song on the cassette tape was "Imagine". A few seconds later, John Lennon belted out the first two lines:

Imagine there's no heaven,
It's easy if you try.

Simon glanced over at the group. They were all wearing frowns. Bobby pushed the girls to the side so that he could lean over the fence.

He shouted, "Turn that blasphemous trash off, you bastard!"

Simon eased the Pontiac backwards. Before putting the car into drive, he turned down the music and sang, "You may say I'm a dreamer, but I'm not the only one".

He was confident Bobby would not know that was a lyric from the song. Bobby swung his legs over the fence and rushed toward the Pontiac. As soon as he reached the Pontiac, Simon hit the gas.

Bobby managed to grab the passenger side door handle, but the door was locked. Simon eased the car through the parking lot. The car was moving slow enough so Bobby could keep his balance and maintain grasp of the door handle but could do nothing else.

A few yards ahead, Simon spotted a car that was backing out on the passenger side. He accelerated and precisely timed it so that if the car continued to back out it would squarely hit Bobby. The backing car braked but not until after its bumper smashed into Bobby's body, pinning him between the two cars.

Bobby screamed, released the door handle, and crumpled to the pavement. Simon slammed on his brakes and exited the car.

Simon's civics teacher, Sharon Creel, witnessed the whole ordeal. She had been helping another student load a box of books in her trunk several yards away. She came running over to the scene of the accident. "Simon, what happened?"

Simon shrugged his shoulders. "I'm not sure. Bobby was angry about something and was trying to get in my car. I didn't want to speed up because I was afraid he wasn't going to let go of the door handle and would be hurt."

The teacher looked over at the young female student who had backed into Bobby. "What about you?"

The student's eyes were wide open, and she was trembling. "I didn't see him, Mrs. Creel."

Bobby lay prone on the pavement. The teacher kneeled to get a better look at him.

"Are you hurt bad, Bobby?"

Bobby didn't answer or even move.

"He's hurt pretty bad. I'm going to rush inside and call 9-1-1."

An ambulance arrived twenty minutes later and carted Bobby off to Methodist Hospital. Simon learned the next day that Bobby had sustained a fractured hip, a broken collar bone, and a concussion. Mrs. Creel corroborated Simon's version of the accident to the police.

Due to his actions, the district court judge revoked Bobby's parole, effective as soon as he was released from the hospital.

Simon smiled when he heard the news.

Imagine there's no heaven. It's easy if you try.

Chapter 11

September 5, 1975, Simon began the fall semester of his junior year at The University of Texas at Austin. He was able to secure a room in Roberts Hall. A placard near the front door of the building indicated that Roberts Hall was built as part of the Works Progress Administration established by the Roosevelt administration after the Great Depression.

Simon unlocked the door to his dormitory room on the second floor of Roberts Hall for the first time and swung the huge wooden door open. He stood a moment and marveled at the small size of the room.

The walls were painted a deep cobalt blue. At the rear, a bank of windows looked out over the courtyard situated behind the circa 1930s dormitory. A small wooden desk sat on the concrete floor against one wall and a single mattress had been left upon some box springs across the narrow room from it.

It was a warm fall day in Austin, Texas. Simon set down his suitcase and ambled over to the forty-year-old windows and eased all three up to let in some fresh air.

The dormitory was without air conditioning and had not been updated with any other modern convenience since it was built. That was the sole reason Simon was able to obtain a private room. Most of the occupants of Roberts Hall were undergraduate students who could not afford the luxury of the newer dormitories on campus.

Simon's parents could pay for him to stay in a newer dormitory, but due to demand, he would have been assigned a roommate. However, this type of arrangement suited Simon just fine. He could get lost in his thoughts, undisturbed by the intrusion of a roommate.

Since the Bobby Hixson experience, Simon had not attempted to use his thoughts to influence anything in the outside world. He still could not grasp why he did not foresee the death of Jimmy Grimes. The more time that passed, the more disturbed Simon became when he thought of the incident.

What have I missed? Every other time, the scenario played out exactly as I thought.

Simon was thankful he had not been goaded to have those thoughts since high school. He had convinced himself that the thoughts only occurred when provoked by others.

* * *

Simon loved his Political Theory class at 3:00 p.m. every Monday, Wednesday, and Friday afternoon. During a class one Friday, Professor Galvin assigned the class the task of reading *Leviathan* by Thomas

Hobbes, to be completed by the following Friday. In part, the book pertained to the structure of government and society. Hobbes did not think fondly of his fellow men. He surmised that nature was essentially "a war of all against all". The only government that could succeed must be strong and undivided in order to control this war.

Simon could not put it down, so he read the entire book in one night. He was enamored with the idea of nature being a war of 'all against all'. This concept so resonated with him that he used it to explain why he had thoughts that could lead to tragic events.

He had no control over being born. Therefore, he reasoned, he could not help it if he was merely a soldier in this war of nature.

Nothing that Professor Galvin presented during the following Friday class discussion swayed Simon from his conviction in this matter. The bell sounded ending class for the day. Simon unzipped his backpack to load his books.

A female voice to his right said, "Who do you think is right?"

Simon jerked his head around and made eye contact with his classmate. The female student was pale and thin, with expressive dark brown eyes and long, straight brown hair. She was dressed in faded blue jeans and a white shirt.

He said, "Excuse me. Were you talking to me?"

She cracked a smile. "Yes. I saw you intensely taking notes during class. I was just wondering who's more accurate, Rousseau or Hobbes?"

Several weeks ago, the topic of discussion in class was the political theory espoused by the Swiss born philosopher, Jean-Jacques Rousseau. Rousseau possessed a much more favorable view of mankind and argued passionately for democracy and equality.

Simon narrowed his eyes. "Hobbes, without question."

She nodded. "I agree. But, listening to the others today in class, we're in the minority."

He rolled his eyes. "I know. They just don't get the true essence of Hobbes."

The female student extended her hand. "By the way, I'm Monica."

Simon shook her hand. "I'm Simon. Nice to meet you."

"Likewise."

He wrinkled his forehead. "I don't think I've seen you before in class."

Monica snickered. "That's because you always sit upfront, and I sit in the back. I have a 4:00 p.m. class in Waggoner Hall. I leave immediately after this class and practically sprint over there to make it in time."

Simon nodded. "That's quite a distance to cover in ten minutes. Aren't you going to be late today?"

She shook her head. "No, the professor told us last Wednesday that the class today was cancelled."

He glanced over his shoulder as students arrived for the 4:00 p.m. class. "I guess we better go, before the next class starts."

They both stood up.

She said, "Where are you heading next?"

He motioned with his head. "The Academic Center to study. What about you?"

"I was going back to my dorm, but do you mind if I tag along with you to the A.C."

Simon's eyes widened. "No, that's great. I usually study on the second floor. It's quieter up there."

Monica smiled. "Perfect."

Four stories tall, the Academic Center was the main undergraduate library on campus. It had an interesting water feature out front that was switched off due to the energy crisis gripping the nation in the mid-1970s. The site of the barren fountain always caused Simon to frown.

Why did I have to attend college at this time when all the fountains on campus are shut down?

That was not the only crisis facing the University of Texas. Simon had signed a contract with the University to eat his meals at the neighboring dormitory known as Jester Hall. The ink was barely dry before inflation shot food prices through the roof. Jester's cafeteria food was barely edible on good days. Due to inflation, the quality and quantity of food offered to students made for a poor dining experience, which further soured Simon with his college experience.

Simon and Monica settled into their seats next to one another on the second floor of the A.C. The second floor was arranged with the bookshelves centered in the middle of the room and row after row of study tables were lined on each side of the bookshelves.

Simon pulled out his Western Civilization textbook and turned to the place where he had left off the previous time he had prepared for that class. As much as he tried, Simon could not concentrate with Monica sitting next to him. A slight hint of her perfume wafted over in his direction.

Simon could sense his anxiety sitting next to Monica and took deep breaths trying to calm his nerves. He had difficulty relating to anyone, especially females. Simon only had a handful of informal dates in his life, which often ended in disaster. His date would either ask to be taken home early or not answer his future phone calls.

He had no dates while at The University of Texas. Attending class and studying defined his life. He maintained a near perfect grade point average for his efforts.

His mother was thrilled with his accomplishments but worried about what she perceived as his lack of a social life. She knew better than to discuss it with him because he always clammed up and refused to talk.

Simon glanced over at Monica, who had the Entertainment page of *The Daily Texan* spread out in front of her.

He whispered, "Studying hard?"

She chuckled. "Busted!" She pointed down at an

advertisement of a movie. "Do you like French New Wave movies?"

He leaned over to look at the newspaper and in his best attempt at French said, "*A bout de souffle!* Yes, I love French New Wave movies, especially this movie, *Breathless!*"

Monica studied his face as if to determine if he were joking. "Really? I do, too!"

Simon felt emboldened. "Would you care to go with me to see it?"

She nodded. "Of course. It starts at 10:00 p.m. tonight in the auditorium downstairs. Do you want to swing by my dorm around 9:30 p.m.?"

"Which is your dorm?"

She pointed to the front of the room. "Dobie. Where do you live?"

Simon smiled. "Roberts Hall, just a few blocks down 21st."

Monica wrinkled her forehead. "I guess I've never been by there. Is it nice?"

He snickered. "To give you an idea, it was built during the 1930s and has never been updated. It doesn't even have air conditioning."

Her mouth dropped open. "I didn't know that any building on campus was not air conditioned."

He smirked. "That's the price you pay for having a single room."

Monica's eyes widened. "You're kidding. You live on campus and don't have to have a roommate."

Simon grinned. "That's correct. It's worth every

drop of sweat in September and October."

She sighed. "I wish I didn't have to have a roommate."

"Why? Do you not get along?"

Monica ran her hand through her hair. "Gwyneth Givens is just so pretentious. I mean she's very pretty and smart, but she's insecure."

He wrinkled his forehead. "Why do you say she's insecure?"

"She acts like she's better than everyone else. But on the inside, I sense she's miserable. Even though she hides it, I know she takes anti-depressant meds."

"It sounds like she has some personal demons she's dealing with."

Monica motioned with her fingers. "She just needles me and belittles me to make herself feel better."

He rubbed his forehead. "This is only the beginning of the semester. Is it possible to change roommates?"

She shook her head. "No, Gwyneth's mother and mine were sorority sisters. They wouldn't understand why their daughters don't get along."

Simon winced. "That's unfortunate."

"Let's change the subject."

He smiled. "Okay, what's the next topic of discussion?"

Her face lit up. "Would you like to know why I sat by you today?"

Simon joked. "I assumed you wanted to be closer to the action, since your 4:00 p.m. class was cancelled."

Monica smiled. "No, it's because I like guys with long blond hair."

He chuckled. "I've let my hair grow long as soon as I enrolled in college. My parents used to make me keep it short. I guess that's my way of rebelling."

She reached over and ran her fingers through a few strands of his hair. "Well, I like it anyway."

Simon felt his cheeks blush. "Uh, thank you."

"It's been fun talking to you, but I need to get back to my dorm. Shall we meet in the lobby of Dobie about 9:30 p.m.?"

He nodded. "Sure, I'll be there."

She gathered her things and winked at him. "Don't be late."

Simon watched as she made her way to the front of the room until she disappeared.

He felt a rush of elation. His spirits were lifted higher than any time in recent years.

She's so cool. I can't believe she's interested in me!

Chapter 12

Simon arrived at Dobie at 9:15 p.m. He had only been on the first level of the complex, which offered several small retail stores and a Schlotzsky's sandwich shop. The lobby of the residential part of the complex was located on the second level.

He lost no time in ascending the stairs and entered the lobby through a rotating glass door. The lobby was much more upscale and nicer than his dormitory, with its discarded overstuffed chairs arranged around the exterior of a worn concrete floor.

In front of him was an empty reception desk and a bank of phones on the wall so that guests could contact residents upstairs. Several people milled around in the lobby, and all but one of the phones were occupied.

Simon wondered why Monica had not given him her phone number. He spotted a grouping of empty chairs that faced a bank of elevators and decided to sit down in one of the chairs to keep an eye on the elevators.

He checked his watch every five minutes. It was now 9:35 p.m. and still no sign of Monica. He flinched when a female voice to his side said, "You have to be Simon."

His head swiveled around until he was facing the source of the voice. Standing a few feet away was a tall, young, blond woman staring at him.

Simon rose to his feet. "Yes, I'm Simon."

The woman sneered at him. "You look like Monica's type."

He wrinkled his forehead. "Who are you?"

"Her roommate, Einstein." She snickered at her insult.

His eyes narrowed. "Where's Monica?"

The woman glanced upward. "She's up in our room. She asked me to tell you to go ahead and she would be along later."

He frowned. "I can just wait."

The woman squinted at him. "Where were you going tonight anyway?"

"Over to the Academic Center to see a French New Wave movie."

She rolled her eyes. "That sounds about par for Monica." The woman whirled around and walked away.

Simon sunk back into his chair and watched as she hurried into an open elevator.

I can see why Monica's doesn't like her. She's such a bitch!

At 9:45 p.m., Simon rose from his chair and all but trotted across campus to the Academic Center. He took the steps down to the basement where the theater was located.

As Simon entered the small theater, which served as a classroom during the day, he scanned the sparse audience hoping to spot Monica, but she was nowhere in sight.

The movie, *Breathless*, started promptly at 10:00 p.m. Although Simon had already seen the movie several times, he always discovered some nuance he had missed in his previous viewings. He sat up straight, stiff in his seat, and stared expressionless at the screen.

When the movie ended, he exited the theatre before the credits finished scrolling. He walked back over to Guadalupe and 21st Street where Dobie was located. He paused on the sidewalk across the street and stared up at the building.

Why didn't Monica come? I suspect Gwyneth is the answer to that question!

Chapter 13

Simon's typical Saturday morning and afternoon were spent studying at the Academic Center. He decided he wanted a change of scenery and opted to study in the main library, which was situated in the iconic University of Texas Tower.

The Tower was notorious for two different reasons. First, the top of it was bathed in burnt orange lights when Texas was victorious in some athletic event. The second reason was a tragedy of colossal proportions.

On August 1, 1966, Charles Whitman ascended to the top of the Tower armed with multiple weapons. From his perch on top of the Tower's observation deck, he shot dozens of people down below, both wounding some and slaughtering others at random, until an Austin police officer killed him.

By the 1970s, the observation deck was open to the public, albeit under tight University of Texas police supervision, preventing anyone from carrying a weapon. The panoramic views from the observation deck made it a still popular destination for students and visitors to the campus.

Simon glanced at his watch. It was noon. He decided to take a break from studying and exited the Tower.

The weather was cool and crisp, abnormal for a late September day in Austin. Simon plopped down on the top of the steps that descended to the plaza below. The plaza was alive with students hurrying back and forth to various destinations on campus.

He watched as a couple of female students ascended the steps leading up to where he sat. As they drew closer, he recognized Monica's roommate. The two young women were engaged in conversation and did not appear to notice Simon sitting only a few feet away staring at them.

He said, "Hi."

The two women whipped their heads around and stared at him. The other woman said, "Who's that?"

Monica's roommate shrugged. "I don't have a clue."

Simon narrowed his eyes. "Don't you remember last night in Dolby's lobby? You came down to tell me that Monica was running late?"

She frowned. "I don't know what you are trying to pull, but I'm not playing along."

Simon cocked his head. "Aren't you Gwyneth?"

Monica's roommate growled, "No, I'm not!"

"This guy gives me the creeps," the other woman said. "Let's get out of here."

Both women scampered up to the front door of the Tower and disappeared inside. Simon waited a few minutes before going back in. He did not want another confrontation.

He took the elevator up to the third floor where

he had been studying and plopped down at the desk.

The more he thought about what had just transpired the angrier he became. No more studying today. He packed up his books and headed back to his dorm.

Simon spent the afternoon and the better part of the night sitting in his dorm room, staring out the window. He ran the encounter with the two women over and over in his head. Simon had not experienced this darkness since his encounter with Bobby Hixson several years ago in high school.

Something must be done!

He climbed into bed and stared at the ceiling of his room. After a short time of tossing and turning, he fell asleep.

Chapter 14

Simon sleepwalked through his Monday classes. Trying not to appear anxious, he waited for his 3:00 p.m. Political Theory class. He arrived early for class and instead of occupying his usual seat toward the front of the class, he opted instead to sit in the back row.

Simon jerked his head around anytime a student entered the classroom. His quick and shallow breathing told him he felt desperate to see Monica.

The bell sounded, signaling the beginning of class, but Monica was a no show. Simon slumped in his chair and doodled with his pen on his spiral notebook.

Why didn't she come to class?

He felt a sudden jolt through his body, as if he had just touched a live wire.

It's happened!

Simon ambled back across campus toward the Academic Center. As he drew near, sirens pierced the air. An ambulance passed in front of him, racing east on campus.

Instead of going into the Academic Center, he wandered over to the mall in front of the Tower.

Several students were gathered in various groups. A few were pointing up at the top of the Tower. The sirens from the ambulance and two City of Austin Police cars drowned out the crowd noise.

Simon spotted a young man standing alone and staring toward the Tower and approached him.

"Hey, what's going on?"

He glanced over at Simon. "I heard somebody just jumped off the Tower."

Simon looked up at the Tower. "Really?"

The man nodded. "Yeah, it looks like he went off the east side."

Simon's eyes widened. "He? It was a guy who jumped?"

The man shrugged. "Hell, I don't know if it was a guy or girl."

Simon rushed back to his dorm room and flipped on the small black-and-white television that his parents had given him before he went off to college. He was hoping to learn more about the Tower suicide.

There was no news yet about the event. The only programs on the three channels he could pick up on his television were either soap operas or talk shows.

Simon flipped the set off and closed his eyes. He could not quite visualize what had happened at the Tower.

The local news at 10:00 p.m. mentioned that someone had jumped off the Tower's observation deck. No mention of the identity of the person was included.

* * *

The next morning, Simon rushed downstairs and grabbed *The Daily Texan* newspaper off the stand in the lobby of his dorm. He sat down in the nearest chair and unfolded the newspaper. The picture on the front page of the newspaper was of two female shoes perched on the edge of the retaining wall surrounding the Tower's observation deck. The article identified the person who jumped as a junior at the University, named Monica Storm.

A chill shot down Simon's spine. He felt nauseated. His heart pounded.

What did I do?

Simon took several deep breaths to try to compose himself. He picked the newspaper off his lap and flipped to the second page of the article. At the top of the page was a picture of Monica Storm from the school's yearbook. Simon was laser focused on the picture.

That's not a picture of Monica! That's a picture of her roommate, Gwyneth Givens! Did The Daily Texan *post a picture of Gwyneth by mistake?*

* * *

Simon made sure at 10:00 p.m. that night to turn on the local news. As he flipped through the channels, every single station flashed the photograph published in *The Daily Texan* as the young woman who plunged to her death off the Texas Tower. He continued to check the university newspaper every morning, searching for any mention of a retraction, but found none.

For the rest of the semester, Simon sat in the last row of his Political Theory class, hoping against hope that Monica would appear. After a few weeks though, doubts crept in as to whether Monica even existed.

He even questioned if he had had the encounter with her roommate Gwyneth Givens at Dolby. She did not seem to recognize him when he spoke to her as she and a friend had ascended the steps of the Texas Tower.

One thing that I'm certain is that the woman who jumped off the Tower was the woman I spoke to on the steps! Did I invent Monica just so I could be provoked?

Chapter 15

February 13, 1980, Simon was a third-year law student at Southern Methodist University in Dallas. He enjoyed the academic aspect of law school but despised the cutthroat competitive nature of his fellow classmates.

Simon speculated that a few of these students would sacrifice their own mothers to one-up their classmates. The atmosphere was highly charged as several academic honors were awarded to students in the final months of school.

Since arriving on campus for the fall semester in 1977, he had befriended only a handful of classmates. Simon sensed that these students befriended him for the sole purpose of benefiting from his superior grasp of the legal concepts. They were always borrowing his notes, which were quite detailed and often provided more insight than what was taught in class.

Of these classmates, Simon's two closest friends were Howard Stoddard and Mika Rawlins. Howard was a tall, strong man with sandy-colored hair and green eyes. He had been quarterback of the football team at Sunset High School in Oak Cliff.

One day, Simon overheard Howard talking

about his high school experience. When he learned that Howard also grew up in Oak Cliff, that created an initial bond. The two young men were friends throughout law school, despite their different personalities.

Simon sat next to Mika Rawlins in both semesters of Constitutional Law. Mika was a petite thin woman with blonde hair that she almost always wore pulled back in a bun. She had a sarcastic wit and appeared to be accepting of Simon's quirky and strange personality. They enjoyed mental sparring games with one another over lunch, regardless of the subject matter.

* * *

April 14, 1980, Mika and Simon were enjoying one of their spirited conversations. Howard walked over and stopped by their table. "Hey guys, I hear they're going to post who made the Order of the Coif this afternoon."

Mika gave Simon a playful punch in the arm. "Simon's a shoe-in. Afterall, the criteria are top grades and excellent research skills."

Simon winced. "I don't know, the last research paper I turned in was flawed."

Howard pulled up a chair and sat down. "That wasn't your fault, Simon. Some jerk tore pages out of several books containing necessary reference materials."

Mika said, "I wonder if the culprit is included in the Order of the Coif."

"Last year, only five students were selected." Simon sighed. "This year, I suspect one of the new members is the one who destroyed the reference books."

Mika nodded. "Yeah, they never did determine who did it."

Howard rubbed his head. "It might be some first-year law student just taking out his frustrations by wrecking the books."

Simon frowned. "I just wish I'd had access to some other law library before the paper was due, but there wasn't enough time."

* * *

After his final class that afternoon, Simon made his way to Storey Hall where the Order of the Coif list was posted. Two students hovered in front of the list pinned to a bulletin board inside a glass enclosure. Simon was taller than both of them and could read the list over their shoulders.

Six names were listed. The last one was Jon Stowers. He was a plump man with a receding hairline who always wore starched white shirts, dress pants and usually a tie. Simon found him to be arrogant and despised him.

He stood and stared at Jon's name for several minutes, seething at the injustice of it. Jon was descended from a family of lawyers, all of whom had attended law school at Southern Methodist University. Several in his family were significant donors to the school. A mock court trial room was even named in honor of his father.

Simon surmised that Jon's wealthy family had pulled some influential strings to get him into law school. Grades were supposed to be confidential, but students talked.

In the few classes they shared, Simon sensed that Jon was winging it. He was ill-prepared and that came through in the faculty's Socratic method of teaching. Jon struggled to answer the simplest of questions.

A voice from behind Simon said, "Admiring the list of the newly minted Order of the Coif?"

Simon shot a glance behind him. Jon Stowers stood there, grinning.

Simon's eyes narrowed. "Some in the group are deserving."

Jon patted him on the shoulder and spoke in a mocking tone. "Simon, I would say better luck next year. But you're a third-year student. So, there won't be a next year."

Simon sneered. "At least I didn't cheat to get in."

Jon's eyes widened. "Are you implying that I cheated? That's a serious accusation." He snickered. "Do you have any proof?"

"Someone destroyed the reference books."

Jon turned to leave. "Poor Simon Steed. No friends

and no Order of the Coif."

Simon's cheeks burned as they flushed bright red. He was furious but said nothing.

Why did he say I have no friends?

As Simon exited Storey Hall, he spotted Mika sitting on one of the benches in the middle of the law school quadrangle. When he approached her, she looked up at him.

"Sorry, Simon."

He plopped down next to her. "You must have seen the list."

Mika nodded. "Yep."

"Yeah, I'm disappointed. But what really angers me is that Jon Stowers made the list."

She rolled her eyes. "I know. There's no way he had the academic credentials. His dad must have made some calls."

Simon sighed. "No doubt."

She said, "I know this is horrible, but I wish something bad would happen to him."

Blank faced; he stared straight ahead. "Maybe it will."

Chapter 16

On May 18, 1980, Simon drove the short commute to the Southern Methodist University Law School. It was a beautiful sunny day in Dallas. He pulled his graduation cap and gown from the front passenger seat of his old Pontiac Lemans.

As he ambled up to the Law Quadrangle, several students were strolling around. Folding chairs covered the lawn leading up to The Underwood Law Library. When the weather cooperated, the graduation ceremony was held outside. Students would walk up the left side of the stairs to the landing of the library, be hooded, and then descend the right side of the stairs to return to their chairs.

Simon searched for both Mika and Howard. Neither were in sight. He went into Lawyer's Inn, which was situated in the Law Quadrangle just opposite the library. Students were invited to use the meeting room inside to change into their gowns prior to the ceremony.

In less than three minutes, Simon slipped into his gown and exited the building. Standing near the front door of Lawyer's Inn was Jean Goolsby, the

Director of Admissions, visiting with a student. Jean took immense pride in getting to know each student during their time on campus. Simon hurried over to where Jean and the student were standing.

"Excuse me, Ms. Goolsby," he said.

Jean whipped her head around and stared at him. "Yes, Simon."

"I apologize for interrupting, but have you seen Mika Rawlins or Howard Stoddard?"

She wrinkled her forehead. "Who?"

"Mika Rawlins or Howard Stoddard."

Jean grimaced. "Simon, can't you just enjoy the day. It's your graduation."

Simon narrowed his eyes. "If you hadn't seen them, you could just say so."

She frowned. "I don't have time to deal with any nonsense today."

His cheeks flushed with anger, but he did not respond. Jean turned back around to face the other student.

Simon shook his head and strolled over to Storey Hall and then scampered up the steps to the landing. He wanted to get a better vantage point to look out for Mika and Howard.

Students filed through the rows and found seats before the ceremony began. Simon sighed and descended the steps and then settled into a vacant seat at the edge in the fifth row.

A. J. Simmons, the Dean of the Law School, approached the podium on the landing of the

Underwood Law Library to commence the ceremony. The landing was two stories high, allowing everyone to have a good vantage point.

Dean Simmons spoke for about twenty minutes and then the hooding of the graduates commenced as the Dean called each student's name in alphabetical order. It took about thirty minutes before he reached the names that began with the letter 'R'.

Simon scanned the crowd, looking for Mika. He anticipated Mika Rawlins' name would be the second or third name called out.

The Dean said, "Edward Raul."

Where's Mika? Her name should be called any second!

Simon was focused on the left set of the steps which the students ascended to reach the landing. Mika was not standing in any group or even by herself.

After hooding Edward Raul, the Dean turned around to the microphone and said, "Sandra Reyes."

Why did he skip Mika?

Simon jolted upright when he remembered that Jean Goolsby did not seem to recognize Mika and Howard's names. He then flashbacked to his encounter with Jon Stowers who needled Simon for having no friends.

This can't be happening!

Simon fell into a trance of sorts until the person sitting next to him nudged him in the arm. "Hey, Simon, you're up."

Simon jerked his head up.

The Dean was staring down at him. "Simon Steed," he repeated, louder.

Simon shot to his feet and scampered to climb the steps. He trembled but managed to get hooded and shake hands with the Dean. He gazed at the crowd as he descended the steps on the right. Everyone appeared to be gaping at him, watching his every move. He made it back to his chair and plopped down as the Dean said, "James Stevens."

Simon closed his eyes.

Please call Howard Stoddard!

Dean Simmons said, "Jon Stowers."

Simon opened his eyes when he heard the name Jon Stowers. He was seething because Howard's name was not called, and he so despised Jon. Simon squinted, watching every move that Jon made ascending the steps.

Jon stopped for a moment at the top of the steps and gave a playful salute to the crowd. Simon's cheeks burned. Dean Simmons hooded Jon and shook his hand. Jon paused again before descending the steps. This time, he bowed from the landing. Simon's eyes were glued on Jon.

Trip on your robe, you bastard!

Midway down the steps, Jon waved at the crowd and lost his footing. He fell headfirst and rolled the remainder of the way down the steps, crashing into the sidewalk below. The crowd gasped.

Simon's frown changed briefly to a smile.

Mika would approve!

A chill fluttered up his spine. He pulled up his left shirt sleeve. His skin was covered in goose bumps.

Why am I experiencing this feeling? Oh my God, I understand now. Mika is short for Monica!

Chapter 17

Since Simon graduated near the top of his class, he secured interviews with the top law firms in Texas. Despite his academic standing, no firm offered him a position. After Simon passed the bar exam in November 1980, he had no choice but to begin his legal career as a solo practitioner.

In order to generate income, Simon hung out in the various criminal courts on Monday mornings, hoping to be appointed as counsel for indigent people charged with crimes for the first time, who now had to appear before the judge. They were appointed an attorney if they could not afford one.

Simon preferred to receive appointments in the District Courts where felonies were tried. The fees paid for representing a defendant charged with a felony were much higher than those for misdemeanor cases.

Although Simon had never intended to go into criminal law, he found he was well suited for this type of work. He was an effective trial lawyer and did not have to worry about his quirky personality. Since he was appointed by the court, his clients had no choice but to accept him.

On Monday April 6, 1983, Simon was assigned to represent Jackie Wayne Timmins, a man charged with murder. The penalties for this charge can include five to ninety-nine years in prison and a substantial fine. Jackie was considered a flight risk by the District Court, so a request for bail was denied.

Simon visited for a short while with Jackie, informing him he would come up and discuss his case with him in the next couple of days. Jackie was then to be transferred back to the Dallas County jail, situated on the top floor of the George Allen Courts Building.

On Wednesday, Simon had a routine motion to file on another case and took this opportunity to go up to the sixth floor and meet with Jackie. He could tell by the pungent aroma when he reached the top floor of the building. A putrid combination of cleaning chemicals and urine permeated the air.

Simon made it through security clearance from the police officer monitoring the jail's reception area. The officer handed him a paper badge with the word 'Attorney' written across the top. Simon snapped the clasp on the collar of his suit coat.

The guard pointed in the direction of several small interview rooms. "They'll bring the prisoner into Room 3. You can wait inside for him."

Simon nodded. "Thank you."

Simon went inside Room 3. It was sparsely furnished with two wooden chairs and a small table. The walls were painted an institutional mint green.

After about ten minutes, Jackie Wayne Timmons appeared at the doorway, handcuffed, with a guard right behind him.

The guard barked, "Sit down" as he shoved Jackie in the back. Jackie plopped down in the chair and rested his elbows on the table, handcuffs rattling. Simon could not help but think that Jackie resembled a young Charles Manson with his dark beard and unkempt brown hair.

As he closed the door, the guard said, "I'll be right outside."

Simon pulled a legal pad out of his briefcase and fished a pen out of his shirt pocket. "Jackie, as you know, Judge Stevens appointed me to represent you."

Jackie stared at Simon but did not respond.

Simon narrowed his eyes. "Are you aware of the crime you've been charged with committing?"

Jackie cracked a slight smile. "Yeah, the cops think I killed that woman."

Simon tapped his pen on the pad. "Yes, you have been charged with murder. Do you understand the elements of what constitutes murder?"

Jackie wrinkled his forehead. "What do you mean?"

Simon stared at his legal pad. "Under Texas law, a person commits criminal homicide if he intentionally, knowingly, recklessly, or with criminal negligence causes the death of an individual. Do you understand what this means?"

Jackie shrugged. "That's a lot of crap I don't

understand. But I'll tell you this, I didn't intentionally kill anyone."

Simon jotted on his pad. "Okay, let's start there. Were you acquainted with the deceased, Elsie Spillers?"

He shook his head. "No."

Simon scratched his head. "Let me rephrase the question. Did you ever have any contact with her?"

Jackie shrugged. "It's possible but not that I recall."

"The indictment against you alleges that your DNA was on the victim's body and on the knife found next to it."

Jackie frowned. "Look, man, I may have been there at the time she was killed. But I didn't do the deed."

Simon narrowed his eyes. "Then how did your DNA end up on the victim and the knife?"

Jackie sighed and paused. "Mr. Jamison made me kill that woman. I didn't want or intend to do it."

"Who's Mr. Jamison?"

"You know, that politician guy."

Simon wrinkled his forehead. "Are you referring to Senator John Jamison?"

He nodded. "Yeah, that's the bastard."

I definitely want to hear this story!

Simon shifted in his chair. "How did Senator Jamison make you do it?"

Jackie shrugged. "I don't know, man. He just got in my head."

Simon sighed. "Did you ever talk to the Senator?"

He shook his head. "No. I can't explain it."

Simon tapped his pen on his note pad. "Would you be agreeable to being evaluated by a psychiatrist?

Jackie raised his hands and crashed the handcuffs down on the table. "Hell no!" he shouted.

The guard heard the noise and opened the door. "Everything all right?"

Simon said, "We're fine, thank you." He looked at Jackie. Simon asked him a few more questions before deciding he was getting nowhere.

This guy's hopeless!

Simon leaned back in his chair. "Okay, Jackie, I think that's all the questions I have for you."

"Are you going to help me, man?"

Simon feigned a smile. "Yes. Just be careful going back to your cell."

Jackie twisted in his chair. "What the hell is that supposed to mean?"

Simon rubbed his chin. "Let's just say that I noticed the guard's gun was not secured in his holster."

Jackie's eyes widened. "Really?"

Simon pushed a button on the wall next to his chair, alerting the guard he had finished interviewing the prisoner. "Yep. Just be careful."

The door swung open, and the guard re-entered the room. "Let's go, Timmons."

Jackie stumbled to his feet and the guard nudged him out the door. The door closed behind them.

Simon leaned back in his chair and closed his

eyes. He mouthed the words, "Now, Jackie."

Scuffling noises came from outside the door and a shot rang out. Simon ambled over and cracked open the door and peered outside. Jackie Wayne Timmons lay face down on the floor in a pool of blood.

I just made a thousand dollars for ten minutes of legal work. Practicing criminal law is turning out to be quite fruitful for me! Thank you, Monica!

Chapter 18

February 2, 1983, Simon scoured the Real Estate Section of the *Dallas Morning News*. He then spotted the perfect house to buy. He had spent the first eleven years of his life in Oak Cliff in that house.

Except for some overgrown shrubs, the picture in the newspaper looked the same as it did when his dad first purchased it just prior to Simon's birth. He called the listing realtor and made a date to see it that afternoon at 3:00 p.m.

Simon pulled around the corner in his 1966 Pontiac Lemans. Due to its age, the Pontiac was in the repair shop almost every week. Regardless, Simon could not make himself trade it in for a newer car.

He had not been in this area of Dallas since that time. The community looked much as it did the day his family moved away in the late 1960s although the trees that lined the streets had matured.

Simon turned right onto Woolsey Drive from Shelmire Drive and eased the Pontiac down the street, checking out his old neighborhood. He parked right in front of his former home and waited for the realtor to arrive, tapping his fingertips against the steering wheel in impatience. The only changes to the landscape in the front yard were the missing gardenia bushes that once lined the left side of the front of the house.

A few minutes later, a white Mercedes Benz SUV pulled up to the curb and parked behind him. A thirty-something blonde woman dressed in a dark gray pantsuit exited the SUV. Simon opened the door and stepped outside as well.

"You must be Simon Steed." She extended her hand. "I'm Sharon Watts."

They shook hands.

He cleared his throat. "How long has this house been on the market?"

Sharon smiled. "It just listed last Thursday. I barely had enough time to meet the deadline for getting it in the Sunday paper."

"So, no one has looked at it yet?"

"You're the first one." She gestured toward the front door. "Shall we go inside and have a tour?"

He nodded. "Sure."

Sharon fumbled with the key and then opened the door. "The house has been vacant for a while."

Simon and Sharon stepped inside the living room. She flipped on the lights.

His eyes darted around the room. "This looks pretty much the same as it did back in the 1960s."

Sharon wrinkled her forehead. "You've been inside before?"

He smiled. "Yes, I spent the first years of my life here."

Her eyes widened. "Really? Well, let's go look around."

They spent the next fifteen minutes walking through the thirty-year-old house. A few improvements had been made over the years, but nothing significant. Newer Formica replaced the kitchen countertops, and fresh paint covered the walls, but the appliances were the same.

They walked down the narrow hallway that led to two bedrooms. Simon and his brother had occupied the room at the end of the hall on the left. His parents had the master bedroom on the right.

When Simon stepped inside his old bedroom, he teared up. The realtor remained at the doorway. He walked over to where the stacked bunkbeds used to be situated. Simon closed his eyes for a few moments to compose himself.

Sharon said, "Are you okay?"

Simon whipped his head around. "I want to put a contract on the house today."

Her eyes lit up. "We can go to the office right now and write it up."

Two hours later, Simon owned the house. He took Monday off to search for two special items of furniture, stackable bunk beds. It was imperative for him that those beds be as similar as possible to the ones he and his brother Steve had slept in as boys.

Simon was about to call it a day, when he decided to check out Sanger-Harris. The department store was located in southwest Oak Cliff in a partially dilapidated shopping center that had seen its heyday in the early 1960s. He located the furniture department on the second floor of the store. The furniture on display looked like it had not changed since the store opened.

Simon ran his finger along the top of a dining table, leaving a visible trail through a layer of dust. He made his way over to where the beds were displayed. Sitting next to the back wall of the store were two bunk beds. They closely resembled the ones from his childhood.

Simon scanned the floor, searching for a sales-clerk. An elderly man with snow white hair rounded the corner. He came to a sudden halt and raised his eyebrows at the sight of a possible customer in the furniture department. The man was dressed in a baggy navy-blue suit, white shirt, and wide plaid tie.

He plodded over to where Simon was standing., then said in a weak voice, "I don't suppose you need any help?"

Simon feigned a smile. "Actually, I do. I'm interested in purchasing a couple of bunk beds near the back wall."

The man's eyes widened. "Really? That's fantastic."

Simon surmised the old man rarely made any kind of sale. He was probably hanging onto employment until he could retire.

* * *

Simon arranged to have the delivery made to his newly purchased home the following morning. He instructed the men where to place the bunk beds. At first, they resisted having to stack one bed on top of the other until Simon offered them twenty dollars each for their trouble.

That night was the first night Simon had spent in his old but now new home since the 1960s. He lay down on the bottom bunk and closed his eyes.

I wonder what Monica has in store for me next?

Chapter 19

October 11, 1982, was a cool crisp day in Dallas. Simon pulled into the parking garage of the Oak Cliff Bank Tower. Earlier that month, he had leased office space in the building on the second floor.

It was a small space consisting of a reception area with a small desk, a typewriter, and two matching client chairs. The carpet on the floor was an industrial dark gray. The only art adorning the white walls were three photographs. Two of them were pictures his dad had taken of Simon hiking in Colorado when he was a young boy.

The other picture contained a ten-inch piece of black-and-yellow crime scene tape. Simon had kept it as a souvenir from when Bobby Hixson drove his car into a fence post in high school, killing his friend, Jimmy Grimms. He thought, if nothing else, it might serve as a conversation piece for prospective clients.

The rent was cheaper in Oak Cliff than downtown Dallas, where he had previously leased office space, and was closer to his home just a few blocks away in the Wynnewood North neighborhood.

Simon had just settled into the chair behind his

desk when the front door to his office opened.

A voice from the small lobby called out, "Mr. Steed?"

Simon stood up and walked across the room and stuck his head out the door. "May I help you?"

A thin dark hair man dressed in blue jeans, work shirt, and cowboy boots stood in the middle of the lobby. "Mr. Steed, I don't know if you remember me. I'm Ray Sanders. You represented me in a DWI case a year ago."

Simon paused. "Yes, Ray, I do remember now. We were successful in convincing the jury you weren't intoxicated."

He nodded. "That's right. Well, I need your help again."

Simon gestured toward his office. "Come on in here. We can talk a few minutes before I have to go to the courthouse."

Simon settled in the chair behind his desk and Ray plopped down into one of Simon's client chairs. Simon pulled a ballpoint pen out of a container on his desk. "Another DWI?"

Ray sighed. "Yeah, I got pulled over again."

Simon narrowed his eyes. "Can you afford my retainer of $3,000?"

Ray fished a checkbook out of his shirt pocket and filled out a check for $3,000 and then slid it across the desk to Simon.

Simon gave the check a brief perusal and then slipped it into the top drawer of his desk. He raised his head and stared at the man. "Okay, Ray, tell me what happened."

Ray rubbed his chin. "Well, I was out with a few of my buddies after work last week."

"What day last week?"

Ray glanced upward as if this would jar his memory. "It was Wednesday. We got off work and decided to have a couple of drinks over at Andrews on McKinney Avenue. After two drinks, I decided to call it a night—"

Simon held up his palm. "You're sure you only had two drinks?"

Ray frowned. "Maybe… maybe it was three. I can't remember, to be honest with you."

Simon tapped his pen on top of his desk. "This is critical, Ray. You need to be absolutely certain how many drinks you consumed."

Ray sank back into his chair. "I can't be sure."

Simon jotted on his legal pad. "When are you due in court to make a plea?"

Ray reached into his pocket and fished out a piece of paper. "This Thursday, at 9:00 a.m." He handed the paper to Simon.

Simon scanned the paper. "You're in Judge Bonham's court."

He scribbled a note on the calendar he kept on his desk. "Okay, Ray, I'll meet you at court on Thursday. I'll talk to the prosecutor when I arrive to see what kind of case they have."

Chapter 20

Thursday morning at 8:30 a.m., Simon arrived at Judge Bonham's courtroom. He spotted Wanda Sterns, a short brunette late thirties woman dressed in a dark gray pantsuit, one of the prosecutors, talking with another defense attorney.

Simon suspected the attorney was there for the same reason as he was. The attorney nodded, but frowned as he walked away from the prosecutor.

Simon approached her. "Wanda, do you have a moment to visit?"

She pursed her lips. "Well now, if it isn't the defense counsel whose clients mysteriously turn into attack dogs."

He narrowed his eyes. "What's that supposed to mean?"

Wanda feigned a smile. "Simon, you have to admit that it's a little strange that several of your clients suddenly attack the prison guards right after they meet with you."

Simon could feel his face flush red with anger. "I don't find that humorous at all."

She patted his arm. "I'm just having a little fun. It breaks the monotony of dealing with defense attorneys all day. Now tell me, how can I be of assistance?"

Simon took a deep breath to compose himself. "I represent a client who has an appearance before Judge Bonham today."

Wanda gestured toward a stack of file folders. "Who's your client?"

"Ray Sanders."

Wanda leaned over and flipped through a stack of files on the table next to her. "Here it is." She opened the file and studied the contents for a few seconds. "DWI," she said.

Simon peered over her shoulder, trying to catch a glimpse of the contents. "Yes, I was curious if any plea agreement was being offered in his case."

He realized prosecutors studied the files before the first court appearance to see which cases should be resolved with a plea agreement, based on the strength or weaknesses of the evidence.

Wanda shook her head. "The case is ironclad. There's no incentive for me to make a deal."

He raised an eyebrow. "What do you have that makes it ironclad?"

"For starters, your client failed a field sobriety test. Second, he refused to voluntarily have blood drawn. Third, a judge granted an order based on probable cause that his blood be withdrawn. Care to hear more?"

Simon sighed. "What was the Blood Alcohol Concentration?"

She smiled. "They clocked him at 0.15, almost

double the legal limit."

He groaned. "Can't you make any kind of deal to plead to a lesser offense?"

"All I can give him is credit for the night he spent in jail after his arrest and lessen the normal community service after probation. However, he must plead guilty today."

Simon rubbed a hand through his hair. "I'll talk to my client."

He exited the courtroom and spotted Ray, dressed in blue jeans, a denim shirt and sport coat, sitting on one of the benches in the hallway. Ray stood up when he saw Simon.

Simon motioned with his hand. "Have a seat. Let's talk a few minutes before we go inside."

Ray said, "Did you find anything out about my case?"

Simon nodded. "Yes, and it's not good. Listen, Ray, they have an airtight case against you."

Ray wrinkled his forehead. "What do you mean?"

"Do you remember them drawing your blood after your arrest?"

He rubbed both his temples. "I do kinda remember that happening. I didn't consent to having it done though."

Simon leaned nearer to Ray. "That's a problem also. They got a judge to allow them to draw blood to see if your alcohol concentration exceeded .08."

"Did it?"

Simon grimaced. "Almost double that."

Ray shifted his weight on the bench. "What do we do now?"

"I asked the prosecutor if you could plead to a lesser offense. Unfortunately, she said no."

"Oh, man, If I'm convicted of a DWI, I'll lose my job."

Simon rubbed his nose. "She said if you plead guilty today, she will give you credit for the night you already spent in jail and reduce your community service requirement."

"What if we take it to trial? Don't we have any possibility of winning?"

Simon sighed. "The only angle we could take is to challenge the chain of custody."

Frowning, Ray narrowed his eyes. "What the hell does that mean?"

"We'd have to prove that some mistake was made from the time your blood was drawn to the time it was tested for alcohol concentration. The odds of being successful are slim to none."

Ray grimaced. "That doesn't sound too promising."

Simon picked up his briefcase. "Well, you have to go plead before the judge one way or the other."

Ray stood up. "Okay, I'm ready."

Simon patted him on the shoulder. "What have you decided to do?"

Ray raised one eyebrow. "You'll find out."

"Okay, Ray. If you want to plead not guilty, I'll represent you at trial. I do want to reiterate that they have a slam dunk case against you."

Simon was uncertain how Ray was going to plea. They waited in the gallery until the judge called his name, then they both made their way to the front of the courtroom.

The prosecutor, Wanda Sterns, was standing to the left side, Ray was in the middle, while Simon was to the right of Ray.

A sharp chill shot down Simon's spine. He was in a mental fog until he realized that Judge Bonham had just asked Ray how he was going to plea. Simon whipped his head around as Ray lunged for the prosecutor. Ray tackled Wanda, throwing her against the wooden jury box.

Judge Bonham shouted, "Bailiff, arrest this man."

A young man wearing a brown guard's uniform came sprinting from the opposite side of the courtroom with his pistol drawn. Simon froze in disbelief as Ray continued to smash his fists into the prone body of the prosecutor. He watched as the Bailiff struck Ray in the back of the head with his pistol handle. After two blows from the pistol, Ray crumbled to the floor.

Judge Bonham stared down at Simon. "Mr. Steed, did you know your client was going to behave in this manner?"

Simon shook his head. "No, your Honor. In fact, I didn't know how he was going to plea. He seemed composed a while ago when I discussed his case with him outside the courtroom."

Judge Bonham raised an eyebrow. "You're telling

me that you didn't know how he was going to plea?"

Simon took his time before he nodded. "That's correct, your Honor... Um, Ray's an interesting character."

He shot a glance over at Ray who lay crumpled up on the floor with his hands cuffed behind him. Two emergency medical responders arrived with a stretcher and rushed over to Wanda Sterns.

The Bailiff and the two men crouched over her motionless body. They checked her pulse and rolled her over onto the stretcher and hurried out of the courtroom.

After they left, Judge Bonham turned back to Simon. "Mr. Steed. The fact that several of your clients acted out in violence after being in your presence has not gone unnoticed."

Simon groaned. "Yes, your Honor. I don't have any explanation for that. I have not provoked them in any manner."

Both men watched as the Bailiff lifted Ray to his feet and escorted him, moaning and unsteady, out the side door of the courtroom.

"I'll take your client's actions today as a plea of not guilty on the DWI charge," Judge Bonham said with a sigh. "He's got bigger things to worry about now."

His tone changed. "All right, now get out of my courtroom."

Simon's stomach was tied in knots when he exited the courtroom. As he walked down the hall, he sensed that everyone was staring at him. He had not felt this way since his first day in junior high school.

Instead of returning to his office, Simon drove the short distance back to his house in Wynnewood North.

He set his briefcase down on his dresser and flopped down on his bed, still dressed in a charcoal gray suit, white shirt, and blue striped tie. Simon lay flat on his back, staring at the bottom of the top bunk bed a few feet above his head. He kept playing what had transpired in the courtroom over and over in his head.

I didn't do anything to provoke Ray? I can't believe the prosecutor and the judge made those comments about my clients acting violently after meeting with me?

He closed his eyes.

Why, Monica? I didn't want to cause Ray any harm. Are you taking over now? Did I do something wrong?

Chapter 21

The following Monday morning at 8:00 p.m., Simon walked into the Dallas County District Court 3. His business bank account was getting low. He felt desperate to get appointed to a new case. From his experience, he knew that Monday was the perfect time to pick up a client or two.

Three other attorneys were sitting in the center of the front row, also waiting to get appointed, so he took a seat one row behind, next to the aisle. Summoning his patience, Simon waited and listened with intensity to Judge Evers talking to a young woman standing before the bench.

The judge was a large bald man dressed in the traditional black robe. The woman wore faded blue jeans, a pink shirt, and a coat that appeared to be a couple sizes too large for her.

After a few minutes, Judge Evers looked up and scanned the courtroom. After about twenty seconds, which seemed like an eternity, his eyes focused on Simon. He frowned but motioned to Simon to approach the bench.

Simon grabbed his briefcase and hurried up to where the young woman was standing.

Judge Evers said in a curt tone, "Mr. Steed, this is Ms. Carol Simms. She has informed me she cannot afford an attorney."

Simon shot a glance over at Carol. She was pretty but unkempt. Her uneven blond hair fell to shoulder length. Carol's face was pale, and she appeared to be wearing no makeup. Her eyes were bloodshot. Simon surmised she had been crying.

"Ms. Simms," Judge Evers said, "Mr. Steed's a criminal defense attorney. I'm prepared to appoint him as your counsel unless you have any objections.

"Do I... uh, do I have to... pay him?"

Judge Evers sighed. "No, I explained this to you earlier. You indicated to me you could not afford an attorney. Dallas County will pay Mr. Steed's fees to represent you."

Carol turned her head to look at Simon. Squinting, she stared at him for a few seconds. "Okay, that's fine. He can represent me."

Simon forced a smile and glanced up at Judge Evers. "Thank you, your Honor."

Judge Evers handed a file down to Simon which contained the formal charge and the paperwork to be completed for him to represent Carol on an official basis.

Simon grabbed the file and turned to face Carol. "Ms. Simms, do you have a few minutes to visit out in the hallway?"

She nodded but did not respond otherwise. Simon opened the door for her to exit the courtroom. He motioned toward an empty bench. "Let's go sit down over there."

After they were settled on the bench, Simon opened the file and took less than a minute to read the charge.

He turned to her and said, "May I call you Carol?"

"Yes." She stuck her legs out straight and wiggled her feet.

"Carol, the county has charged you with felony prostitution. I assume you understand why this is a felony charge instead of a misdemeanor."

She sat up straight and shook her head. "No, it's been a misdemeanor every other time."

He sighed. "That's correct. For the charge to be a felony, you must have been convicted three or more times for prostitution."

Carol gasped. "That's not right!"

Simon studied her face. "Are you sure? It will be simple for me to find out."

She frowned. "I guess I could have been convicted three times before. I can't remember."

Simon pulled a legal pad and pen out of his briefcase. "Tell me what happened the night you were arrested."

Carol swallowed. "My guy told me not to come back until I made five hundred dollars—"

"Excuse me for interrupting." Simon tilted his head sideways. "Who's this guy?"

She shook her head. "I can't say anything about him."

Simon wrinkled his forehead. "Why not?"

Her eyes darted around the hallway, then she whispered, "He'll hurt me if I say."

He tapped his pen on the legal pad. "Okay, go on with your story."

She sighed. "Last Saturday night, he dropped me off in a parking lot next to Harry Hines. I waited until he drove out of sight and then I began working. A bunch of girls were working that night, so I had a lot of competition. I was only able to get one guy to pick me up before a cop in an unmarked car pulled over and arrested me."

Simon scribbled on his legal pad. "When a man picks you up, where do you go?"

Carol turned up her nose. "There's this flea bag motel just off Royal Lane. My guy has an arrangement with the sleazy manager there."

"Do you recall the name of the motel?"

She shrugged. "No, I never have noticed a name. It's always dark."

He looked up from his legal pad. "Where on Harry Hines did the arrest take place?"

Carol scratched her head. "I think it was just north of Royal Lane."

"When the officer pulled over to the curb, was anyone else around?"

"No, not at that time. The other girls were working in a different area. I was all by myself."

Simon wrote on his legal pad. "Tell me every detail of what happened. For example, did you wave at him or otherwise try and get his attention?"

She smirked. "I may have given the cop a slight wave. He pulled his car over and rolled down the front passenger side window. I approached the car and leaned on the car and looked inside. He smiled at me and asked if I was working. I smiled and said that it depended on him. He patted his coat pocket and said he had three Benjamins in his wallet if I was interested. I nodded but didn't say anything. That's when he jumped out of the car and arrested me."

"Did the officer ask whether you were working at the direction of someone?"

Carol shook her head. "No, he didn't ask and I sure as hell didn't bring up my guy."

Simon gave her shoulder a gentle pat. "I know you don't want to talk about this guy, but it's critical to your defense. You know you're facing a possible lengthy prison term, since this is a felony case this time."

She sniffed and her eyes watered up. "I understand. But I'm afraid of what he might do."

Simon thought she looked so fragile and vulnerable.

"Listen, Carol, if we can show you were coerced into prostitution, then we have a viable defense to the charge. To do that, though, you need to tell me about this guy."

The same as before, Carol turned her head left and then right, surveying the hallway.

"What do you need to know?"

He tapped his pen on his legal pad. "Let's start with his name."

"His name's Frank Rogers."

Simon jotted on his legal pad. "How did you meet Frank?"

She sighed, "I was working one night. When Frank pulled his car over to where I stood, he asked me if I would like a date. He drove me to that same run-down motel. Instead of having sex, he beat me up pretty good. When I begged him to stop, he said he would if I worked for him from now on."

"What happened next?"

Carol twisted a strand of her hair around one finger. "Frank told me to go home and take care of my face and be ready to work in a week. As I gathered up my things to leave, he grabbed my arm, squeezing it hard. I thought he was going to beat me again. I started crying. He warned me that if I told anyone about him, he would kill me." Gulping, she paused to compose herself.

Simon looked up. "What happened then?"

"He turned me loose and let me go. I returned to Harry Hines the next week and began working for him."

He leaned forward. "What kind of car does Frank drive?"

She sniffed. "A black Camaro."

"Do you know his license plate number?"

Carol shook her head. "No. It begins with the letters LST. I don't remember the numbers."

Simon jotted on his legal pad. "Does Frank know where you live?"

She sighed. "I don't think so. The only time that I see him is at night on Harry Hines."

He opened the file he had received from Judge Evers and studied the contents for a few seconds. "You must enter a plea next Monday. I'll talk with the prosecutor at that time and see what I can learn about your case. In the meantime, don't go back down to Harry Hines."

Her eyes widened. "But I have to make some money to pay rent."

Simon studied her face. He was confident she was telling the truth. "How much do you need for rent?"

"I'm short by about two hundred dollars."

He fished his wallet out of his pocket and pulled out three hundred dollars and handed it to her.

Carol's mouth dropped open. "What do I have to do for this?"

Simon narrowed his eyes. "Two things. First, get yourself some food for the week. Second, do not... I repeat, do not... go down to Harry Hines. Agreed?"

She nodded. "Yes, thank you."

He slipped the file and legal pad in his briefcase. "That's all I have for now. Do you have any questions for me?"

Carol tucked the folded bills into her small purse. "What time do you want me down here next Monday?"

"Can you be here by 8:00 a.m.?"

"Yes."

Simon stood up. "Carol, I'll see you next week. Please be careful."

She stood up, stretched, and then ambled down the hall. Simon watched her until she disappeared around the corner.

I hope I didn't make a huge mistake by giving her money.

The more he thought about what had just transpired, the better he felt about what he did on behalf of Carol. Some of the darkness lifted.

Chapter 22

Monday night at 8:00 p.m., Simon slid behind the wheel of his 1966 Pontiac Lemans and switched on the ignition. He worried that driving such an old car might bring unwanted attention. Nevertheless, Simon wound through downtown Dallas and made his way over to Harry Hines Boulevard.

Simon had not driven on the street in several years. Traffic was light this time of night until he reached Mockingbird Lane.

As he drove north, a series of strip clubs and adult nighttime establishments popped up on both sides of Harry Hines Boulevard. Cars going either direction crawled along at a snail's pace. He did not know why he felt compelled to come to this area tonight.

What if I see Carol working the streets? Do I stop and try to convince her to go home?

As Simon eased up the street, he scanned the area for any sign of Carol. When he drew nearer to the intersection of Royal Lane and Harry Hines Boulevard, he spotted several women dressed in scanty, revealing outfits, hanging around near the intersection.

Korean-owned businesses consisting primarily of small retail stores populated the immediate area. They were all closed so the parking spaces in front were vacant, except for a few cars parked with the motors running.

"So, this is where some of the women make their connections with prospective customers," he muttered.

He proceeded farther north on Harry Hines. Most of the businesses were closed except for a service station on the east side and an adult bookstore on the west. Simon glanced down at his fuel gauge. He was driving on fumes.

He pulled the Pontiac alongside one of the pumps. As he was filling his tank, Simon noticed a man talking to two women on the side of the building.

One of the girls spotted Simon looking at them, because she pointed at him. The man whipped his head around and squinted at Simon.

The hose on the pump clicked, indicating that Simon's car tank was full. He placed the nozzle back in the pump's holster. Out of his peripheral vision he caught sight of the man, standing behind the Pontiac a few feet away.

The man said, "Nice ride, man."

"Thank you." Simon fumbled for his keys. "It gets me around."

The man was stout and muscular, wearing a leather jacket and faded blue jeans. He sported a scruffy beard and scraggly dark hair. When he stepped closer, he touched the top of the Pontiac's trunk. "I bet it does. I don't suppose you would be interested in selling it?"

Simon shook his head. "No, I've had it since high school. I'm not about to part with it now."

The man shot a glance over at the two women. "In that case, would you like to have a pretty girl riding shot gun in it?"

Simon opened the door to his car. He could not remember if the passenger side door was locked. "No but thank you."

Simon slid into the driver's seat. Before he could close the door, the man grabbed the handle. "Hold your horses, pal. Don't be rude. Just meet one of my girls."

He shouted, "Judy, come over here."

A chill shot down Simon's spine, but he sat frozen in place.

The woman walked over and stood next to the man.

"Judy, say hi to this man. If you're nice, he might take you for a ride in his sleek old car."

In a squeaky high voice, the woman said, "Hi, mister. Would you like a date?"

Simon turned his head to inspect her. She was dressed in a gold-sequined miniskirt and tight-fitting white blouse. Dark makeup around her eyes was smudged. Her hair was dyed platinum blond with an inch of dark brown roots exposed.

Simon took a deep breath to calm himself. "Hi,

Judy. Thank you for your offer. But I promised my wife I'd be right home."

She frowned. "Frank, he's not interested."

Simon's eyes lit up. His mood shifted to a dramatic degree. At once, he felt emboldened, and laser-focused his eyes on the man.

"You must be Frank Rogers."

Frank released the door handle and took a step backwards. "Do I know you?"

Simon feigned a smile and shook his head. "No, but I sure recognize you."

Frank's eyes widened. "Who the hell are you anyway?"

Simon closed his door and rolled down his window just a crack. "Frank, let's just say I am someone's guardian angel."

Frank grabbed Judy's arm and yanked her backward, as if preparing to run. "Let's get out of here Judy. This guy's crazy and may be dangerous."

"By the way, Frank," Simon shouted, "You have a nice ride yourself. I love the Camaro."

Before firing up the Pontiac's engine, Simon watched Frank and the two women disappear behind the building. Simon turned the ignition key and eased to the end of the lot. A small driveway led to an alley just behind the building.

I wonder if Frank's parked in the alley?

A few seconds later, a black Camaro came roaring down the alley and vanished behind the building next door to the service station. Simon followed the

Camaro down the alley and was able to memorize the license plate.

The Camaro turned west onto Royal Lane and Simon turned east and pulled the Pontiac over to the curb. He popped open his glove box and fished out a pen and paper so he could jot down the license plate number before he forgot it. LST 1977

What to do about Frank?

He took a deep breath.

No Monica, please not tonight. I don't want to harm the women if they're in his car.

Chapter 23

The following Monday, Simon took the elevator up to the fourth floor. When he rounded the corner, he found Carol sitting on a bench, twitching and shaking, just outside of Judge Evers courtroom.

He approached her and sat down beside her. "How are you doing, Carol?"

She wore the same outfit she had on last Monday. Simon guessed that it may be the only nice clothes she owned.

Her eyes darted around. "I'm okay. I'm just nervous."

"I understand." He smiled for a few seconds, then relaxed his facial muscles. "Now I must ask you. Did you do what we discussed last Monday?"

Carol nodded. "Yes, I didn't go to work."

"That's good. I need to tell you something before I go talk to the prosecutor."

She wrinkled her forehead and cocked her head a bit. "What do you need to tell me?"

Simon sighed. "I met Frank last Monday night."

Her eyes widened as she gasped, "Are you serious? You met Frank?"

"Yes, it was purely by accident. I was filling my car up with gas on Harry Hines when I spotted a man talking to two women near the service station—"

Carol twisted sideways and grabbed his forearm. "You were on Harry Hines last Monday night?"

He nodded. "Yes, I decided to drive down near where you were arrested."

"But why?" She released her grip and sank back against the wall.

Simon shrugged. "To be honest with you, I don't know. Maybe I was checking to see if you were working."

She narrowed her eyes. "I told you last week I wasn't going to work."

"I know. I apologize." He paused. "I was worried about you."

Carol leaned forward. "Okay, tell me what happened with you and Frank."

"As I said, I was filling my car up with gas. I drive this old classic car. That may be what got Frank's attention. Before I knew it, he was standing behind my car within a few feet of me. He asked me if I was interested in selling it and I told him no."

Simon shifted his position. "When I tried to leave, he grabbed ahold of my door handle. He insisted I meet one of the women. To avoid trouble, I agreed to meet her but remained in my car. A woman named Lucy came over and asked if I was interested in a date.

Carol tapped her hand on the bench. "I know

Lucy. Is she still that hideous platinum blonde?"

He nodded. "Yes, that pretty well describes her. Anyway, when I told Lucy I wasn't interested, that's when she addressed Frank by his name. Something came over me and I felt compelled to asked him if he was Frank Rogers."

She snorted. "I bet he didn't like that."

Simon smiled. "No, he was surprised. So, I decided to further rattle his cage. When he asked how I knew his name, I told him I was someone's guardian angel."

Tilting her head back, Carol snickered. "That's priceless."

"Frank, Judy, and the other woman hurried behind the service station. I followed them down the alley in my car and was able to get his license plate number."

She patted the back of his hand. "That's incredible. You're lucky he didn't shoot you."

Simon groaned. "Does Frank carry a gun?"

"Yes," Carol said as she nodded, "he keeps it in his coat pocket at all times."

He glanced at his watch. "I need to go visit with the prosecutor about your case. Let's go inside the courtroom. You can sit in the public seating area while I talk to the prosecutor."

Stephanie Willis, a tall blond woman dressed in a light gray pantsuit and white blouse, was prosecutor in this court. Simon had tried a couple of cases against her and thought she was tough but fair.

She stood reading a file, leaning against the jury

box, then glanced up as he drew near. "What can I do for you, Simon?"

He set his briefcase down next to him. "I represent Carol Simms and need to visit with you about her case."

Stephanie flipped through a stack of files and pulled one up and opened it. Simon watched as she studied the contents.

She raised her eyes and stared at him. "She's charged with Felony Prostitution."

He nodded. "Yes, but there are some extenuating facts that have a bearing on the charge."

She arched one eyebrow. "Enlighten me."

"Ms. Simms has a defense to the charge," he said in a firm tone. "She was coerced into prostitution by a man named Frank Rogers."

Stephanie smirked. "She has three priors for prostitution. Are you implying she was coerced all four times?"

Simon shook his head. "No, she admits the other three were her fault. Is there anything in the record to indicate that the arresting officer ever inquired if she was coerced?"

Stephanie flipped through the contents of the file. "There's nothing in the file one way or another. Without visiting with the arresting officer, all I can do for you today is make a plea offer of misdemeanor prostitution."

"Stephanie, I have personally witnessed this guy forcing a woman to prostitute herself."

She squinted at him. "I'll tell you what I'll do. Call my office and get on my schedule so we can meet and discuss it in further detail. I don't have time now."

Simon picked up his briefcase. "If I can't convince you of her defense, will you still at least allow her to plead to a misdemeanor offense?"

Stephanie sighed. "Yes, we have a deal."

He smiled. "Thank you, Stephanie."

Simon walked to the back of the courtroom and motioned for Carol to join him outside in the hall. They sat side by side on a bench. She was laser-focused on Simon trying to anticipate what he was going to tell her.

He gave the area a quick scan before speaking. "Carol, if you plead guilty today, the prosecutor will reduce the charge to a misdemeanor."

She slumped a bit, using her body language to express her disappointment. "No, I thought you had some kind of defense."

"Let me explain. The prosecutor has agreed to meet with me more in-depth about your case. When we meet, I'm going to tell her all about Frank and how he physically threatened you to work for him. If I can convince her, I think she will consider dropping the case against you."

Carol perked up. "When are you going to meet with her?"

He leaned forward. "I'm going to call her office to schedule an appointment as soon as I get back to mine later this morning. Do you have a phone where you live?"

She nodded. "Yes."

He fished a pen out of his shirt pocket. "What's your number?"

"972-355-7887."

"I'll give you a call as soon as I learn something." He jotted down her number. "How are you doing on money?"

Carol frowned. "To be honest, I'm running pretty low."

Simon pulled his wallet out of his coat pocket and handed her five hundred dollars, placing it in her palm. "This should last you for a while."

She cocked her head. "Why are you doing all this for me?"

"I'm not entirely sure myself. My helping you seems to be helping myself." He slipped his wallet back into his coat pocket. "That probably doesn't make sense to you either."

Carol seemed to be hanging on to his every word. "Well, thank you."

Simon glanced at his watch. "Let's go before Judge Evers and enter a plea of not guilty."

Chapter 24

Wednesday morning at 10:00 a.m., Simon took the elevator up to the fifth floor of the George Allen Courts Building. He was able to arrange an appointment with Stephanie Willis for 10:15 a.m.

This was Simon's first visit to the fifth floor where the Dallas District Attorney and the various prosecutors kept their offices. The floor resembled the other floors of the building, except courtrooms were on the first four floors, with the Dallas County jail on the sixth floor. Closed wooden office doors that looked identical lined the hallway. Besides each door was a plastic plate bearing the name of the prosecutor who occupied the office.

Simon located Stephanie's door and waited just outside. At precisely 10:15 a.m., he knocked on the door.

A voice from inside said, "Come in."

Simon opened the door and stood in the doorway. Stephanie's desk was covered in stacks of files and papers. She was hovering over an open file that was resting on her desk right in front of her.

Without looking up, she said, "Have a seat, I'll be

with you in just a minute."

After a couple of minutes, Stephanie looked up and stared for a moment at Simon before speaking. "Oh yes, you wanted to talk about the felony prostitution case. What's the defendant's name?"

Simon leaned forward in his chair. "Carol Simms."

She flipped through a stack of folders on the side of her desk and fished one out. She opened it and glimpsed inside. "As I recall, you indicated your client has a defense to the charge."

He nodded. "That's correct. A guy named Frank Rogers physically threatened her if she did not work for him."

Stephanie sneered, "Simon, I hear this excuse all the time. She has three prior convictions. Was this Frank involved with those as well?"

"No, just this one case."

She shifted in her chair. "How do we know this Frank even exists?"

Simon sighed. "I met him at a service station Monday night last week on Harry Hines Boulevard."

Her eyes widened. "What were you doing down there?"

"I was appointed to represent Ms. Simms that morning. She promised me that she would stay away from Frank until Monday of this week when she had to make a plea. I even gave her some money so she could make rent and buy some food."

Stephanie tapped her pen on the desk. "I assume you went down to Harry Hines to see if she kept her promise."

Simon rubbed his nose. "I suppose that was the case. I can't say with a hundred percent certainty the reason I went down there. Anyway, as I was cruising north just beyond Royal Lane, I spotted a service station. This prompted me to check my fuel gauge. I was driving on fumes, so I pulled in to fill my car up. While pumping gas, I noticed a man talking to two women on the side of the building. One of the women must have seen me looking at them. A few seconds later, the man was standing a few feet from me."

"Was this man Frank Rogers?"

He nodded. "Yes. I drive this 1966 Pontiac LeMans. The man wanted to know if I would be interested in selling it. I told him no and tried to leave. He insisted I meet one of the women. To avoid trouble, I agreed. She then asked me if I wanted a date. When I told her no, she said, 'Frank, he's not interested.' For some reason, I felt emboldened and asked him if he was Frank Rogers. That seemed to spook him, and he and the women piled into his car parked behind the service station. I followed him a short distance down the alley so I could get his license plate number."

Stephanie snickered. "You're lucky the guy didn't shoot you."

"I know. Ms. Simms just told me he does carry a pistol."

"What's Frank's license plate number?"

Simon fished a piece of paper out of his pocket. "LST 1977. He drives a black Camaro."

She jotted on a legal pad. "I'll have the police check this guy out."

He leaned back in his chair. "Thank you, Stephanie. If you find out he's trafficking women, will you drop the charges against my client?"

Stephanie raised an eyebrow. "If he's engaged in trafficking. Then, I'll drop charges contingent upon Ms. Simms agreeing to testify against him."

Simon groaned. "I don't know if she will agree to testify. She's terrified of him."

She exhaled, "I'm sure she's terrified of him, but that's the deal."

He stood up. "I'll talk to her."

"Simon, why have you taken such an interest in Ms. Simms?"

Simon wrinkled his forehead. "What do you mean?"

She leaned forward and rested her elbows on the desk. "You lend your client money and then attempt to track her down at night. That's more than just representing your client."

He scratched his head. "I don't know. For some reason I can't explain, it makes me feel better about myself."

Chapter 25

Wednesday afternoon at 2:30 pm, Simon flipped through the massive Yellow Pages phone book that he kept in the bottom drawer of his desk. He located various Dallas County social work providers that specialized in helping victims of sex trafficking.

Simon spoke with several of the providers before selecting one. He made an appointment for 11:00 am, Friday morning. After hanging up the phone, Simon leaned back in his chair and closed his eyes.

My God, I hope Carol will agree to go to the appointment.

He picked up the phone receiver and dialed Carol's phone number. After the third ring, Carol answered in a soft voice. "Hello."

Simon leaned back in his chair. "Hello, Carol, this is Simon Steed. Do you have a few minutes to talk?"

"Uh, yeah... yes, sure, now... it's fine."

He sensed she was very anxious but also keen to hear what he was about to say. "I met with the prosecutor this morning about your case. I told her all about Frank and how he threatened you into working for him. Also, I told her about my encounter with Frank last week down on Harry Hines."

"What did she say?"

Simon picked up a pencil off his desk and tapped the erasure on top of his desk. "Well, I think that episode convinced her to at least have Frank investigated. I gave her Frank's license plate number."

"Is she going to do anything about my case?"

"Yes, she agreed to drop the case against you if they corroborate our stories that Frank engages in trafficking women. There's one condition, though."

"What's that?"

Simon dropped the pencil and rubbed his nose. "You have to agree to testify against him if he goes to trial."

Carol released a heavy sigh. "I don't know if I can. He'll kill me if I do."

"Carol, you must agree to testify if you want to avoid the felony prostitution case. There's no getting around it."

There was nothing but silence at the other end of the line.

"Carol, are you still there?"

"Yes... Okay, I'll do it."

Simon smiled. "Good. I also have something else I want to discuss with you."

Another sigh. "What's that?"

"You have to give up being a prostitute. If you continue down this path, you'll either end up dead or in prison."

Sniffing at the other end of the line. *Is Carol crying?*

"I don't know how to do anything else," she said, "in order to make money."

Simon leaned back in his chair. "Carol, I contacted several different social worker organizations in Dallas County. They specialize in helping victims of sex trafficking. In fact, I made an appointment for you this Friday at 11:00 am. Will you at least agree to keep the appointment?"

"I don't know."

"What if I picked you up and took you to the appointment. Would you agree to go?"

"Why are you doing this for me?"

Simon rubbed his chin. "You are not too much younger than I am. Most of your life is ahead of you. I want you to have an opportunity to be happy."

"Are you happy, Mr. Steed?"

His eyebrows shot up as he paused. "That's an excellent question. All that I can truthfully say is that I have every opportunity to be happy."

"I will go to the appointment."

"Wonderful, I'll see you Friday morning."

Friday morning, Simon called Carol two hours before her scheduled appointment. He wanted to make sure she had not changed her mind and also to get her address. Simon felt relieved she was still willing to go to it.

At 10:15 a.m., he pulled his Pontiac into the parking lot of the Rambler Apartments located just off Denton Drive and Royal Lane. The apartment buildings needed more than updating and freshening, since they seemed to be about thirty years old. They were rundown and unkempt. Weeds several feet high lined the splintered and uneven sidewalks.

He located her apartment and tapped on the front door. After a few seconds, the door cracked open, and Carol peered out before unlatching the lock.

As she was opening the door, the sunlight lit up her face. Carol was wearing a simple dress, no make-up, and her hair pulled back in a ponytail. Although she was only a few years younger than Simon, she looked even younger.

"Good morning, Carol."

She smiled. "Good morning, Mr. Steed."

"Please just call me Simon."

She stepped outside and then locked the door behind her. "Okay, I'll call you Simon."

He pointed with his right hand. "That's my car right over there."

Carol stopped in her tracks. "That's what you drive?"

Simon nodded, "Yelp. It's a 1966 Pontiac LeMans. My dad bought it for me when I was a senior in high school. I've been driving it ever since."

He opened the passenger door for her, and she slid into the seat.

While Simon started the car, she said, "I don't think anyone has ever opened my door before."

He winked at her. "Well, I'm sure it won't be the last time."

Once they arrived and Carol checked in, Simon waited for her in the small reception area of the facility. He wondered if she would be receptive to whatever advice or therapy she was receiving.

Simon checked his watch. It was noon. He had not been in his office since yesterday morning. It was imperative for him to go to court in the morning so he could try to pick up some court appointed cases. His bank account was sinking fast to a dangerous level.

The door swung open behind the reception desk, and Carol and a mid-fifties bald man wearing navy slacks and white shirt appeared in the doorway.

"It was nice to meet you, Carol," the man said. "I look forward to our next session. As we discussed, please contact Ms. Bowles first thing on Monday morning so she can help find you a job."

She nodded, "Yes sir, thank you."

Carol smiled when she spotted Simon.

He stood when she approached him. "How did it go in there?"

"Okay, it's just a lot to take in."

He opened the front door for her to exit the building. "Would you like me to take you to lunch?"

She shook her head. "No, you've done enough for me. Please just take me home."

"Okay, I'll take you home then."

Simon glanced over at her as he drove her back to her apartment. She sat motionless, staring straight ahead. "Can you tell me how your appointment went?"

Carol whispered in a shaky voice, "They want to change everything about my life. I've so much to think about."

He pulled the Pontiac into the parking lot of her apartment complex and eased into the space nearest where her unit was located.

She looked over at him. "Thank you for all you've done for me. I really appreciate it, even though..." She stopped mid-sentence.

"Even though what?"

Carol shook her head. "It's nothing." She leaned over and gave him a light kiss on the cheek.

Simon watched her as she wove her way up the dilapidated sidewalk toward her apartment.

I wonder what Carol was going to say?

Chapter 26

Simon unlocked the door to his office as his phone started ringing. He hurried over to his desk and grabbed the receiver. "This is Simon Steed."

A woman's firm voice said, "Hello, Simon, this is Stephanie Willis. I wanted to let you know that Frank Rogers has been formally charged with trafficking."

Simon picked up a pen from the top of his desk. "Great! Has he entered a plea?"

"Yep, just this morning. He pled not guilty and requested a jury trial."

He scribbled on a legal pad. "Any idea when it will go to trial?"

She sighed. Her voice now sounded tired. "His attorney filed a motion for a speedy trial. It's scheduled on the docket two weeks from next Monday."

"Is he out on bail?"

"Unfortunately, yes."

Crossing and uncrossing his ankles, Simon shifted in his chair. "I assume you still want Carol to testify."

"Absolutely. I don't have an airtight case without her testimony. I'm going to give her a call right now to schedule an appointment, but I wanted to give you a heads-up."

"Thank you, Stephanie."

After the call ended, Simon leaned back in his chair. He laced his fingers together and stretched his arms up. His knuckles popped as he staired at the ceiling.

Carol's not going to be happy about this!

* * *

Simon turned off the television. He was sick of watching sitcoms on all three major networks. Simon could not quit thinking about what Carol started to say. Over and over in his head, he ran the conversation they had on the way home from the appointment this morning.

He grabbed the receiver off the wall phone in his kitchen and dialed Carol's number. After letting it ring ten times, he hung up.

Simon snatched his car keys off the kitchen counter, hurried outside, and slid behind the wheel of his Pontiac. He drove the short distance to downtown Dallas and made his way to Harry Hines Boulevard. Similar to the last time Simon ventured down this route, the cars crawled along in both directions as he neared Royal Lane.

As he drove north, he surveyed both sides of the street. A blond woman waved at him. Simon was not certain why, but he slowed down and eased the Pontiac into the parking lot. As he drew nearer, he rolled down his window.

The woman was dressed in a tight-fitting, red mini dress. She wobbled on her seven-inch-high heels over to where he was parked. When the woman arrived, she leaned on his car and poked her head inside the window. Her eyes were bloodshot, and the smell of alcohol and cigarettes emanated from her breath.

She said, "Hey, baby, would you like a date?"

He forced a smile. "No, I'm looking for Carol. Have you seen her tonight?"

She squinted at him. "I don't know any Carol, but I'm way better than her."

Simon shifted his car into drive. "Thank you. I'm sorry to have bothered you."

After he spun away from the woman, Simon glanced in the rearview mirror. The woman still stood where he had left her with a puzzled expression on her face. He turned back onto Royal Lane and continued north.

Then Simon pulled the Pontiac into the same service station where he had met Frank. His eyes darted back and forth, searching for Carol.

All the spaces in front of the service station were vacant. At the side of the parking lot, a man knelt while putting air into a rear tire of a pickup truck. Simon took a right turn back onto Harry Hines Boulevard and drove farther north. When he reached the overpass of Interstate 635, he made a u-turn and headed south.

Just north of the Royal Lane intersection a group of three women clustered alongside a black Honda minivan. Simon assumed they were negotiating with the occupants.

He drove farther south and came within a few yards of the Walnut Hill Lane intersection when he spotted Carol. She had on the same simple dress that she had worn that morning to her appointment. She was talking to someone on the passenger side of a red Jaguar F-Type parked in front of a closed retail business.

Simon pulled in the space next to where Carol stood. Neither Carol nor the occupants of the Jaguar seemed to notice him. He rolled down his window.

"Hi Carol, I've been looking all over for you. Your mother's worried sick about you."

She jerked her head around. Her mouth dropped open. "Simon, why are you here?"

He feigned a smile. "To make sure you get home safely."

A man's voice from inside the Jaguar said, "Hey buddy, she's busy. Get the hell out of here while you can."

Simon left his car running but jumped out of the Pontiac and walked up behind Carol, acting calm. He reached into his pocket and pulled out of his wallet a State of Texas Bar Card, which all attorneys licensed in the state of Texas possess. He flashed it by the occupant of the Jaguar and hoped the man did not have time to see that it was just a bar card.

"Sir, I'm an officer," Simon said. "If you don't want me to ruin your night, you'll back your beautiful Jaguar out of that parking space and get out of here."

The man wrinkled his forehead. Simon speculated the guy was trying to determine if he was bluffing or not. A few seconds later, the Jaguar eased backwards. Carol and Simon watched as the car made a right turn onto Harry Hines Boulevard.

Carol said, "What was that officer B.S. all about?"

He chuckled, "Well, it's true that I'm an officer. All licensed attorneys in Texas are officers of the court."

She rolled her eyes. "I'm asking you again. Why are you here?"

He gave her arm a gentle touch. "I could ask you the same question. You don't need to be doing this anymore. May I please take you home?"

Carol nodded.

He started his car and glanced over at her. "Does Frank know you're out here?"

She sighed. "I don't think so."

Simon drove the short distance to Carol's apartment and parked. The two of them ambled down the sidewalk toward her apartment. While she fumbled with unlocking her front door, he took his wallet out of his coat pocket.

She stopped jingling the keys and turned to stare at him. "What are you doing?"

Simon grabbed all the dollar bills inside and tucked them inside her purse.

Her eyes widened. "Why? Did you want to come inside?"

Simon shook his head. "No, I just want you to be safe."

Carol whispered, "Thank you" and kissed him on the cheek.

He said, "Did you talk to the prosecutor about testifying against Frank?"

She pursed her lips. "Yes, she called. I told her I would have to think about it."

Simon groaned. "Carol, it's not an option. If you don't testify, she's going to charge you with at least misdemeanor prostitution! Do you understand?"

Carol nodded but lowered her head and wouldn't look him in the face. "Yes, I understand."

He clasped both shoulders. "Please let me call her tomorrow and tell her you'll testify."

She looked up at him. "Okay."

"Thank you. I promise to be there in court to support you."

Chapter 27

Three weeks after Frank Rogers filed a motion for a speedy trial, a jury was seated for his trial on Monday, January 4, 1983. Simon had just returned from making the rounds to the various courts, trying to get appointed counsel for indigent clients. He made it just in time to watch both attorneys make opening arguments from where he sat in the back of the courtroom.

Lynne Ellis was prosecuting the Dallas County District Attorney's case. She was a petite brunette, perhaps in her upper twenties. Lynne wore the standard charcoal gray pantsuit with a white blouse. As Simon later discovered, she was just hired and had passed the bar exam a mere three months earlier.

Simon was disappointed that Stephanie Griggs did not prosecute the case herself.

Frank Rogers was represented by Sloan Sutton, a prominent Dallas criminal defense attorney. He was a thick heavy-set man with slicked back, dark brown hair that was graying at the temples. Sloan wore a dark blue suit, starched white shirt with diamond cufflinks, and a red tie.

Simon had never met him but knew him by

reputation. Hardly a month went by without Sloan making the headlines of the *Dallas Morning News* for representing some well-known individual.

Dressed in the usual black robe, Judge Evers peered down over all the proceedings. The jury was composed of six men and six women. Three of the men and two of the women were Black. The rest of the panel was White.

As is customary, Lynne went first and gave an effective portrayal of Frank as a demonic predator and serial sex trafficker of innocent women.

Simon's eyes were glued on Frank. He was dressed in a charcoal gray suit, white shirt, and gray tie. His hair was combed back, away from his forehead, and his face clean shaven.

Frank's appearance in court was completely different than the grungy unkempt character who had approached Simon at the service station on Harry Hines Boulevard. Frank smiled as Lynne gestured in his direction while she described his role in trafficking young women.

At the conclusion of her opening argument, Sloan paused several seconds for dramatic effect before rising to his feet. Simon studied him as Sloan made eye contact with every single person on the jury several times. He had a deep baritone voice with a strong Texas accent. Sloan referred to himself as a 'country lawyer'.

His portrayal of Frank Rogers was the exact opposite of Lynne's description. He painted Frank as a successful entrepreneur and businessman who happened to be in the wrong place at the wrong time. His arrest was the simple result of overzealous police officers trying to clean up an ugly part of Dallas by any means possible.

Sloan presented himself well as charismatic and charming. Simon was laser-focused on the jury because they appeared to be hanging on to his every word. He wondered how the jury would react to Carol. She was not scheduled to testify until tomorrow morning.

"Ms. Ellis," Judge Evers said, "you may call your first witness."

She said, "I would like to call Detective Mike Spradlin to the stand."

Detective Spradlin was dressed in a charcoal gray suit, white shirt, and navy blue tie. He had chiseled features and closely cropped brown hair. Simon guessed him to be in his mid-thirties.

Lynne said, "Please state your name and job for the record."

"Mike Spradlin, Detective," he barked, "Vice Unit, Dallas Police Department."

"How long have you been in this role?"

"Ten years as a detective and three years in the Vice Unit."

Lynne shot a glance over to the jury. "Detective, can you tell us what happened the night of March 11, 1983?"

He nodded. "Yes, I was working the northwest

Dallas area on night patrol. I always make certain to check the area on Harry Hines Boulevard several times every night. At 11:00 p.m., I was driving north near the Royal Lane Intersection when I spotted what appeared to be man and a woman arguing in the parking lot. I decided to investigate so I pulled my car into the parking lot a few feet away from them."

"What kind of car were you driving?"

The detective shifted in his chair. "I was driving a Ford Expedition."

"Marked or Unmarked?"

He sighed, "Unmarked."

Lynne gazed down at her legal pad. "So, there's no way that the man or woman would've known you were a Dallas detective, is that correct?"

He nodded, "That's correct."

"What happened next?"

"I exited my car and asked them how they were doing this evening. The man indicated that they were doing fine. He appeared to be sizing me up and then asked me if I was looking for some fun."

Lynne bounced in her chair. "Let me stop you there." She pointed towards Frank Rogers. "Is that man the defendant?"

Detective Spradlin shot a quick look over at the defense table. "Yes, he's the man."

"Thank you. Please continue."

Detective Spradlin rubbed his chin. "I smiled and asked him to tell me some more. The defendant gestured with his head toward the woman and said she's one of the best. She's got a clean room nearby. I glanced over at the woman. She appeared to have been crying because her makeup was all smudged and her eyes were bloodshot.

"I said, 'Young lady are you all right?' She nodded but didn't say anything. The defendant then screamed at her and told her to tell me the price. She whispered that it would be three hundred dollars. That's when I identified myself and informed them that they were under arrest for prostitution."

Lynne tapped the table with her pen. "How did they respond?"

Detective Spradlin groaned. "The defendant tried to convince me that he was innocent and was trying to help the woman."

"And what happened next?"

He smiled. "I told him it looked to me like he was trafficking this woman."

Spradlin scrutinized the jury box as if inspecting its members before he continued. "A squad car pulled up about that time and two officers exited and I told them that the defendant and the woman were under arrest. The officers cuffed them and took them to the Dallas County Jail."

Lynne paused and studied her legal pad. "I pass the witness, your Honor."

Sloan stood up. "Detective Spradlin, you indicated you have been a Detective with the Dallas Police Department for ten years, that correct?"

Detective Spradlin nodded. "That's correct."

"And the last three years you have been in the Vice Unit, correct?"

"Yes."

Sloan leaned back in his chair. "So, is it fair to say that all your focus as a Vice Unit detective is on enforcing this area of the law?"

Detective Spradlin shifted in his chair. "I think that's a fair statement."

"I suppose I would be correct in assuming that prostitution falls in the purview of Vice Unit?"

Detective Spradlin smirked. "Of course, it does. It and narcotics are about ninety percent of what I focus upon."

Sloan jotted on his legal pad. "You testified earlier that you arrested the defendant in a parking lot just off Harry Hines Boulevard. Why were you patrolling that area of Dallas?"

"There's a lot of prostitution on Harry Hines near where I arrested the defendant."

Sloan glanced over at the jury. "So, you were there specifically to make an arrest for prostitution, correct?"

Detective Spradlin nodded. "If I was suspicious and had probable cause that a crime was being committed."

"You testified earlier that you thought the defendant and a woman were arguing. That prompted you to pull your car over and investigate, correct?"

Detective Spradlin sighed. "Yes."

Sloan cleared his throat. "Would two people who

appeared to be arguing be probable cause that a crime was being committed?"

Detective Spradlin pursed his lips. "No, but it was suspicious enough that it warranted investigating."

"You said earlier that the woman's makeup was smeared, and she appeared to be crying. Did the woman say she and the defendant had been arguing?"

Detective Spradlin shook his head. "No."

Sloan chuckled. "So, your purpose for investigating proved to be unfounded, correct?"

Detective Spradlin rubbed his chin. "I guess that's correct."

Sloan leaned back in his chair. "You arrested the defendant under a charge of Compelling Prostitution, correct?"

"That's correct."

"Can you enlighten us with the elements of that crime?"

Detective Spradlin rubbed his chin as if that would help him remember the elements. "Compelling Prostitution is when an individual causes someone by force, threat, coercion, or fraud to commit prostitution."

Sloan leaned forward. "You have agreed your assumption that the man and woman were arguing was unfounded. So, there was no argument but somehow the defendant forced, threatened or coerced the woman to commit prostitution. Isn't that true? That's sounds a little farfetched?"

Detective Spradlin sneered. "The defendant

screamed at her to tell me the price. That's the way these kinds of guys operate."

Sloan smiled at the jury. "Did he physically force her or threatened her into prostitution?"

"Not in so many words. But having been down this road so many times before, it's implicit in the way both were behaving."

Sloan snickered. "Implicit, huh. I pass the witness."

Lynne peeked down at her legal pad. "Detective Sloan, I want to clarify for the jury your encounter with the defendant. Who initiated any discussion about you being offered the woman's services for money?"

Detective Spradlin jerked his head toward Frank Rogers. "The defendant asked me if I wanted to have fun."

"What was the woman doing while he was offering her services?"

"She was just standing there, staring at me."

Lynne shifted in her chair. "Did she say anything?"

He sighed. "Not until he screamed at her to tell me the price. As I stated earlier, she said it would be three hundred dollars."

"So, she didn't speak until she was forced to speak by the defendant?"

Detective Spradlin nodded. "That's correct."

She glanced over at the jury. "In your professional opinion, did the defendant sound threatening?"

Sloan jumped up. "Objection, Detective Spradlin

is not an expert witness."

Lynne shot back. "As a detective, he has to deal with threatening as well as violent people all the time."

With a slight wave of his hand, Sloan said, "I believe a psychiatrist would be a more appropriate expert witness."

Judge Evers said, "Sustained."

Lynne grimaced. "Let me reframe the question. As a reasonable human being, did you think the defendant was threatening the woman?"

"Yes, definitely."

Lynne said, "Pass the witness."

As he came out from behind the defense table, Sloan said, "You indicated earlier that the defendant tried to convince you he was helping the woman, is that correct?"

Detective Spradlin frowned. "Yes, that's correct."

"How did he say he was trying to help her?"

"The defendant said he saw her leaning against a car, crying. That's when he pulled his car over next to her and asked if she was okay."

Sloan raised an eyebrow. "Didn't you ask her the same question?"

"Yes, I noticed her makeup was smeared."

Sloan returned to the table and glanced down at his notes. "You testified you were driving an unmarked car, correct?"

Detective Spradlin leaned back in his chair. "That's correct."

"You also testified you didn't think either the man or woman knew you were a detective with the Dallas Police Department, correct?"

Detective Spradlin nodded. "That's correct."

"So, as far as the defendant and the woman were concerned, you could've been a bad guy, isn't that correct?"

Detective Spradlin shrugged. "I suppose so."

Sloan shrugged, raising his arms halfway, palms up. "I would assume that Harry Hines Boulevard at that time of night is not a safe place, correct?"

"It's a high crime area. A lot of prostitutes frequent this area which also attracts an unsavory crowd."

Sloan sighed. "Do uniformed officers and marked squad cars routinely patrol this area?"

Detective Spradlin nodded. "Yes, it's a high priority for the Northwest Dallas Division."

"So, it's possible that, if the defendant thought you were a bad guy, he might want to try any means possible to stall until the police drove by, correct?"

Detective Spradlin scowled. "I think that is highly unlikely."

Sloan smiled at the jury. "That's all the questions I have for Detective Spradlin, your Honor."

Simon thought Sloan did a nice job on cross examination, but believed the prosecution had the upper hand. He decided to exit the court and return to his office. While in route, his thoughts drifted toward Carol.

I hope she holds up in court tomorrow. God, I hope she shows up!

Simon could not remember a time when he had felt this good about life. Monica had not provoked him in a long time.

Chapter 28

Early Tuesday morning, Simon thought about calling Carol to see if she might want him to take her to the George Allen Courts Building. Judge Evers would handle some other business in his courtroom before resuming the trial.

He arrived at Judge Evers' courtroom at 9:00 a.m. There was no sign of Carol outside of it, so he stuck his head inside.

Several attorneys were stirring around, trying to get the ear of Stephanie Willis to make some deal on behalf of their clients. Lynne was seated at the prosecution's table. She was flipping through her legal pad. Simon surmised she was going over her questions for the direct examination of Carol Simms.

He exited the courtroom and sat on one of the benches and waited. At 9:20 a.m., Carol emerged from an elevator at the end of the hall. She ambled down the hallway. She was dressed in a solid light pink dress, with her hair pulled back in a ponytail. Her eyes darted back and forth as she approached where Simon sat.

He sprang to his feet and smiled. "How are you doing, Carol?"

Her hands were fidgeting. "To be honest, I'm scared to death."

Simon gestured toward the bench. "Have a seat. We'll visit until they need you inside."

"Is Frank inside the courtroom?"

He shrugged. "I went inside briefly to look for you but didn't see him either."

Her eyes got wide, and she flinched. Simon glanced over. Frank and Sloan were walking in their direction.

Simon whispered, "It's going to be okay. Try to stay strong."

Before entering the courtroom, Frank stopped in his tracks, sneering at Carol. "You can't be serious. You're going to testify against me?"

Sloan said, "Let's go inside, Frank."

Frank then made eye contact with Simon. He froze for a second. "This is priceless! Carol and her guardian angel."

Sloan grabbed Frank's arm. "Let it go, Frank."

The two men entered the courtroom. Simon looked at Carol. She stared at the floor, shaking.

Simon put his arm around her. "He can't harm you anymore. You're safe."

The bailiff opened the door and called out, "Is a Carol Simms here?"

Simon gave her a gentle nudge. "It's time." He helped her stand up and move toward the door.

"Are you Carol Simms?" the bailiff said.

She nodded. "Yes sir."

The bailiff opened the door. "Ms. Ellis has called you to testify."

Simon followed them inside. Only a few people sat as spectators inside the courtroom. He selected a seat on the front row to give himself the best vantage point. Carol was sworn in and the direct examination began.

Lynne said, "Could you please state your full name for the record?"

Carol's voice was barely audible. "Carol Ann Simms."

"Ms. Simms," Judge Evers said, "you're going to have to speak a lot louder than that for everyone to hear you."

She nodded. "Yes sir."

Lynne said, "Ms. Simms, or may I call you Carol?"

"Yes ma'am, Carol."

Simon guessed that Lynne wanted to address Carol by her first name to make her feel more comfortable.

"Carol, are you married?"

Carol shook her head. "No, ma'am."

"What do you currently do to support yourself?"

Carol took a deep breath. "I'm in a support program which is teaching me some vocational skills and providing me therapy. I don't really have a real job yet."

Lynne leaned forward. "What is the nature of this support program?"

Carol glanced at Simon. "It's a non-profit organization that provides counseling for victims of sex trafficking and helps them get their lives back together."

Lynne looked over at the jury. "Why did you seek the help from this type of organization?"

Carol grabbed a tissue from a box sitting next to her and dabbed her eyes. "Because I am a victim of sex trafficking."

"How are you a victim of sex trafficking?"

Carol sighed, then said, "I was forced to prostitute myself."

Lynne shifted in her chair. "Who forced you?"

Carol peeked at Frank. "Frank Rogers beat me and forced me to work for him."

"Will you point at the man that trafficked you?"

Carol was trembling but managed to point in the direction of the defense table.

Lynne said, "Please let the record reflect that the witness has identified Frank Rogers." She glimpsed down at her legal pad. "When did you first meet Frank Rogers?"

Carol shifted her gaze toward the ceiling. "A couple of months ago."

"Okay, can you tell us how he forced you?"

She nodded, "Yes, he told me that from now on, I was going to work for him. He then beat me up pretty bad, so I would know he was serious. I couldn't work for a week until I healed from the bruises. The very next time I worked, I had to give him half of what I made."

Lynne sighed as she scanned the front row of

the jury. "And did he threaten or beat you after you started working for him?"

"Yes, he regularly threatened me and told me I needed to make more money. If I didn't, he was going to beat me up again."

Lynne studied her notes. "Where did you work for Frank?"

Carol swallowed, "I worked over on Harry Hines Boulevard near the Royal Lane intersection."

"Why did you select that particular area of Dallas to work?"

"Because that's where most of the men cruise in their cars looking for working girls."

Lynne ran her hand through her hair. "How do you get these individuals' attention to actually stop?"

Carol frowned, then her facial muscles twisted into more of a wince. "I wear something sexy, and I subtly wave at them to get their attention. It's not difficult to get them to pullover."

"What happens after an individual pulls over to where you are?"

"We talk for a while and then I tell them my price. If they agree, we go to the Miramar Motel nearby."

Lynne looked down at her legal pad. "Do you always take them to the same motel?"

She nodded. "Yes, Frank has an arrangement with the manager there."

Simon glanced at the jury. They appeared to be laser focused on Carol.

"What kind of arrangement?"

Carol shrugged. "I'm not really sure. I think he gets a discount on the room if I keep bringing customers there."

Lynn raised an eyebrow. "Is this a nice motel?"

Carol wrinkled her nose. "It's filthy and rundown."

"As far as you know, are you the only person working for Frank?"

"No, there are two other women."

Lynne jotted on her legal pad. "Do you know the names of these other two women?"

Carol shook her head. "Not their real names. I just know their street names."

"Do you have a street name as well?"

Carol grimaced. "Yes, Frank told me to tell customers that my name was Bridgett."

"Did he tell you why he thought you should go by the name of Bridgett?"

She nodded. "Yes, he said it sounded sexy."

Lynne stared at her legal pad for a few seconds. "I pass the witness."

Sloan stood up and said, "Ms. Simms, I assume you don't mind if I call you Carol as well."

"No sir. I don't mind."

Sloan smiled. "Thank you, Carol. You stated earlier that you met Frank Rogers a couple of months ago, is that correct?"

She nodded. "Yes sir."

"Where exactly did you meet him?"

Carol cleared her throat. "On Harry Hines Boulevard."

His eyes widened. "Do remember where on Harry Hines Boulevard that you first met?"

"Yes sir. It was in a parking lot near the Royal Lane intersection."

"I see. Isn't it true, that you testified earlier that men cruise this particular area in search of working girls?"

Carol grabbed another tissue from the box next to her. "Yes sir."

"Is it accurate to say that you were one of those women working that night and looking for customers?"

She dabbed her eye with the tissue. "Yes sir."

Sloan glanced over at the jury as he sat down again. "Prior to meeting Frank Rogers, how long have you been a prostitute?"

A tear ran down Carol's face. Simon wondered if she was going to hold up.

"About a year, I guess."

Sloan bounced in his chair. "So, you were pretty experienced in this line of work before meeting Frank, is that correct?"

She whispered. "Yes."

Judge Evers said, "Ms. Simms as I said earlier, you're going to have to speak loud enough to be heard throughout this courtroom."

Carol looked up at him. "My answer was yes."

"You testified earlier," Sloan said, "that Frank forced you to prostitute yourself. But the truth is, you were already prostituting yourself before you met him, correct?"

"But that was different. I worked for myself then."

Sloan tapped on the tabletop with a pen. "Let me take a step back here. On the night you met Frank, isn't it true that you waved at him when he was driving north on Harry Hines Boulevard near the Royal Lane intersection?"

Carol shrugged. "I don't remember exactly all the details."

"You stated earlier that your method for getting men to stop was to wear something sexy and wave at them in their cars, correct?"

She nodded. "Yes sir."

Sloan shifted in his chair. "Do you recall what you were wearing that night?"

Carol shook her head. "No sir."

"But it was something sexy to attract men, correct?"

Lynne jumped up. "Objection, she has already answered that she doesn't remember what she was wearing."

Judge Evers said, "Sustained. Ask your next question, Mr. Sutton."

Sloan grimaced, "Somehow you were able to get Frank's attention because he pulled his car into the parking lot where you were standing, correct?"

"Yes sir."

"When Frank parked his car, he rolled down the window and asked how you were doing, isn't that correct?"

Carol looked up toward the ceiling. "That sounds

about right."

Sloan rubbed his nose. "You said that you would be doing much better if he was looking for a date, correct?"

She gave a slow nod. "I think so."

Sloan leaned forward. Isn't it true that Frank said he wasn't certain what he wanted to do?"

Carol shrugged. "I don't remember exactly what he said."

"Didn't you then tell him that a date with you would cost $300?"

She sighed. "I can't recall what happen."

Sloan glanced over at the jury. "Regardless, you eventually got into the car with him, isn't that right?"

Carol nodded. "Yes sir."

"You wouldn't have gotten in the car with him if you hadn't agreed upon a price for services, correct?"

"That's correct."

"Where did you go?"

She sniffed. "I wanted to go to my usual location, but Frank insisted we go to the Miramar Motel."

Sloan smiled, then his expression faded into a sneer. "What is your usual location?"

Carol appeared to be sinking in her chair. "My apartment."

Sloan's left eyebrow shot up. "You usually take your customers back to your apartment?"

She tilted her head to one side and lifted her shoulder in a half-shrug, as if to recoil from his question. "Yes sir."

"But you agreed to go to the Miramar Motel with Frank, correct?"

"Yes sir."

"He didn't force you, did he?"

Carol shook her head. "No sir."

Sloan looked down at his legal pad. "I pass the witness."

Lynne said, "Tell us what happened after Frank, and you arrived at the Miramar Motel."

Carol rubbed her right eye. "We talked for a little while. Frank was nice to me at first and then told me that I was going to work for him from now on. When I refused, he started hitting me in the face with his fists. I begged him to stop."

She grabbed another tissue and dabbed both eyes. "He finally stopped when I agreed to work for him."

"There were numerous occasions that he threatened to beat you, correct?"

Sloan jumped up. "Objection, leading question."

Judge Evers said, "Sustained."

Lynne grimaced, "Did he ever threatened or beat you again?"

Carol nodded, "Yes."

"Do you recall how many times?"

"Almost every time I saw him."

Lynne said, "Pass the witness."

"I assume in your profession," Sloan said, "that you run into all types of individuals, is that correct?"

Carol nodded. "That's correct."

Sloan shifted in his chair. "Some are probably not too nice to you, are they?"

Carol paused before answering. "I try to avoid that type of person."

"You testified earlier that Frank was nice to you at first, correct?"

"Yes sir."

Sloan cocked his head. "Have any of your customers been nice to you at first and then changed their behavior?"

Carol looked down at her lap. "Sometimes that happens."

"Carol, prostitution is illegal in Texas, isn't it?"

She heaved a big sigh. "Yes sir."

Sloan jotted on his legal pad. "Is it fair to say that, when you're committing a crime like prostitution, some risks are involved?"

Carol wrinkled her forehead. "I'm not sure I understand your question."

"By risks, I mean there will be certain hazards to the job, such as people threatening or not treating you well, which would be different if you were doing a normal legal job, correct?"

Lynne jumped up. "Objection, Counsel's question calls for speculation."

"Sustained." Judge Evers said. "Please rephrase your question."

Sloan chuckled. "Thank you, your Honor, I believe that's all the questions I have for the witness."

Judge Evers looked down at Carol. "You may step down, Ms. Simms."

Simon watched as Carol made her way through the courtroom. Her shoulders were slumped, and her cheeks were flushed. Simon stood up and met her as soon as she entered the public area of the courtroom.

"You did just fine," he whispered. "Let's go visit a few minutes in the hall."

They sat on one of the benches just outside the courtroom.

"How are you doing?"

Her lower lip quivered. "Terrible. That attorney made me look so cheap and bad."

Simon put his arm around her shoulders. "It's over now. You won't have to testify anymore."

She just stared straight ahead.

"Would you like me to drive you home?"

She nodded. "Yes, please."

Simon wanted to watch the remainder of the trial but felt obligated to take Carol home. He speculated that it would conclude with closing arguments in the morning.

After dropping off Carol, Simon returned to his office. As soon as he sat down, the phone on his desk rang.

He grabbed the receiver. "Hello, this is Simon Steed."

A woman's voice on the phone said, "Hello Simon, this is Stephanie Griggs. Do you have a moment to visit?"

Simon picked up a pen off his desk. "Yes, how can I help you?"

"I assume you are aware that Frank Rogers is currently being tried on a charge of Compelling Prostitution?"

"Yes, I have watched part of it. In fact, I saw my client Carol Simms testify today."

A sigh came through from the other end. "You were in attendance today?"

Simon rested his elbows on his desk. "Yes, and I saw the detective who arrested Frank Rogers testify earlier."

"That's unfortunate. Lynne Ellis wants to call you as a witness."

He groaned. "Really? But I'm Carol's attorney. Don't you think that would prejudice my testimony?"

"I realize that, but she wants you to testify about your encounter with Frank Rogers that evening on Harry Hines Boulevard. Carol's testimony was a little weak since it was brought up that Carol was a sex worker before she met this Rogers character. Lynne thinks your testimony would bolster the argument that Frank is trafficking several women."

Simon scribbled on his legal pad. "I watched Carol's testimony in court. I'm sure the defense will object to my testifying."

"Lynne wants to risk it all the same."

He sighed. "When does she want me at court?"

"Tomorrow, 9:00 a.m. in the morning."

"Okay, I'll be there."

Stephanie said in a terse voice, "I'll let her know."

Simon leaned back in his chair. "May I ask why

you didn't try this case yourself?"

"Lynne needs the experience. Why do you ask? Do you not think she's doing a good job?"

"Let's just say, I believe you would have done better."

Chapter 29

The following morning, Simon made his usual rounds at the George Allen Courts Building, trying to pick up court-appointed cases from the various District Courts. He arrived at Judge Evers' courtroom at 9:00 a.m. and walked inside.

Stephanie Griggs and Lynne Ellis stood in front of the prosecution's table, facing the rear of the courtroom. Stephanie waved at Simon and motioned for him to come inside the bar area. She introduced him to Lynne and told him to take a seat at the table next to her.

Sloan Sutton and Frank Rogers were already seated at the defense table. Simon glanced over at them and watched as Frank leaned over and whispered into Sloan's ear. After a few moments, Stephanie exited through a side door.

Judge Evers said, "The bailiff is bringing the jury in."

With the exception of Judge Evers, everyone rose to their feet and remained standing until the panel was seated.

He peered down at Lynne. "Ms. Ellis, you may call your first witness."

"I would like to call Simon Steed to the stand."

Simon ambled up to the witness stand and settled into the chair. After the court reporter swore him in, Lynne began her questioning. "Could you please state your full name for the record?"

Simon glanced over at Frank, who was glaring at him.

"Simon Joseph Steed."

"And what do you do for a living, Mr. Steed."

He sighed. "I'm a criminal defense attorney."

Sloan jumped to his feet. "May we approach the bench?"

Judge Evers waved for Sloan and Lynne to come forward.

Sloan said, "Your Honor, this witness has been sitting in the public gallery throughout this trial. It's likely that whatever testimony he gives has been prejudiced by what he has already heard."

Judge Evers said, "Ms. Ellis, do you have any response?"

She nodded, "Yes, the witness will testify about events completely unrelated to any of the testimony heard so far."

Judge Evers said, "All right, I'm going to let the witness testify but if there is any overlap, I will intervene immediately."

Sloan said, "I would like the record to reflect my objection to this witness testifying."

After shifting his glasses down the bridge of his nose and bending his head forward, Judge Evers peered over at the court reporter. "Let the record reflect the defense counsel's objection."

Sloan and Lynne returned to their respective tables.

Lynne looked up at Simon. "Mr. Steed, have you ever seen the defendant before this trial began?"

Simon nodded. "Yes, I saw him one night in the parking lot of a service station near the intersection of Royal Lane and Harry Hines Boulevard."

She glimpsed down at her legal pad. "Did you and defendant engage in any conversation?"

"Yes, I was filling my car up with gas when I saw the defendant talking to two women on the side of the building. I think they spotted me looking at them. That's when the defendant walked over to where I was parked. I drive a 1966 Pontiac Lemans. The defendant commented on my car and then inquired if I was interested in selling it. I told him I wasn't interested.

"He then called a woman named Judy over to where we were. She asked me if I wanted a date. I told her no and then she turned to the defendant and addressed him as Frank. That's when I suspected that he might be Frank Rogers. I said something to the effect that 'you must be Frank Rogers'."

Lynne leaned forward. "How did you happen to know his name was Frank Rogers?"

Simon cleared his throat. "My client told me about him."

"And who is this client?"

He sighed. "Carol Simms."

Lynne glanced at the jury. "In your opinion, was Frank controlling of this woman?"

"I'm not sure I understand the question."

"Let me rephrase. Do you think the woman would have come over and offered to have a date with you if Frank had not been there?"

Simon shrugged. "He did seem to be the one in charge."

"What happened after you identified the defendant as Frank Rogers?"

"I think it must have spooked him because his demeanor turned nervous. He and the woman hurried over to where the other woman was standing and all three disappeared behind the building. I started my car and drove over to where I last saw them. A few seconds later, a black Camaro came speeding down the alley, so I followed it until it reached Royal Lane."

Lynne tapped the table with her pen. "Why did you follow the Camaro?"

Simon glimpsed over at Frank. "I wanted to get his license plate number."

"And did you get it?"

He nodded. "Yes, it is LST 1977."

Lynne studied her notes for a few seconds. "I pass the witness."

Sloan said, "Mr. Steed, you testified that you're a criminal defense attorney, correct?"

"Yes."

"You also stated that you represent Carol Simms.

Why would Ms. Simms have the need for a criminal defense attorney?"

Simon groaned. "She was charged with a crime, and I was appointed to represent her."

Sloan raised an eyebrow. "What type of crime?"

"It had to do with prostitution."

"In fact, she was charged with a felony prostitution, correct?"

Simon pursed his lips. "That's correct."

Sloan cocked his head. "What made it a felony charge instead of a misdemeanor?"

"She has three prior convictions for prostitution. Since a fourth charge was brought, she can be charged with a felony."

"I see." Sloan managed a frosty smile as he looked over at the jury. "Carol Simms has been convicted already three times for prostitution."

Judge Evers said, "Mr. Sutton, do you have a question for the witness?"

"Yes, your Honor," Sloan said. "Mr. Steed, you sat back there in the public gallery yesterday, listening to your client's testimony, correct?"

Simon nodded. "Yes, however, I had no idea until yesterday afternoon that I was going to be called as a witness. I wouldn't have been in court if I had known."

"As her attorney, you have to do what's in her best interests, correct?"

Simon narrowed his eyes. He did not know where Sloan was going with this question.

Sloan leaned forward. "Is it fair to say that you wouldn't have testified today if it wasn't in the best interests of Ms. Simms?"

"I would have preferred not to have testified, but I was requested to do so by the District Attorney's office."

"Did anyone in the District Attorney's office threaten to subpoena you if you refused to testify?"

Simon shook his head. "No, but I assume I would have been subpoenaed if I had refused to testify."

Sloan smiled. "So, you voluntarily testified, which was beneficial to your client, correct?"

Simon sighed. "I voluntarily testified."

Sloan shifted in his chair. "Let's go back to the night you said you first met Frank Rogers. You stated you were pumping gas into your car near the intersection of Harry Hines Boulevard and Royal Lane, correct?"

Simon nodded. "Yes, that's right."

"We've heard testimony from your client, Carol Simms, that Harry Hines and Royal Lane is a location frequented by prostitutes and their clients. Why were you down there at night?"

Simon felt a pit in his stomach. "I'm not sure exactly why I went down there."

Sloan raised an eyebrow. "You're not certain?"

"That's correct. I believe I wanted to check and make certain Carol was not there."

"Did you see Carol Simms that night?"

He shook his head. "No."

Sloan glanced at the jury. "I pass the witness."

Lynne said, "I have no more questions for Mr. Steed."

"You may step down, Mr. Steed," Judge Evers said.

Simon felt dejected, even deflated. Everyone on the jury must have been staring at him as he made his way out of the courtroom. While Simon was curious to watch the remainder of the trial, he decided to go to his office.

That was a total disaster. My testimony did nothing to bolster the case against Frank.

Chapter 30

Wednesday morning, Frank filed a motion on behalf of a client in one of the misdemeanor courts. At 9:00 a.m., he arrived at Judge Evers' courtroom.

Stephanie Griggs was seated at the defense table, talking to a man dressed in a dark suit and tie. Lynne Ellis was nowhere in sight.

Simon sat down in the front row of the public gallery. After a few minutes, the man left, and Simon stood up and entered the bar area. Stephanie appeared to be studying the contents of a file that was in front of her on the table.

"Excuse me, Stephanie."

She said, "Just a moment" and continued what she was doing. After a couple of minutes, Stephanie looked up and a puzzled look took over her face. "What can I do for you, Simon?"

"I wanted to see how the trial is going?"

She frowned. "It's over."

Simon wrinkled his forehead. "What do you mean it's over? I thought Lynne was going to put an officer on the stand to corroborate my testimony about Frank's license plate."

"No, Lynne felt the case was falling apart, so she decided to work out a plea deal with the defendant."

Simon rapped on the table with his fist. "You've got to be kidding. Why did she feel it was falling apart?"

She sighed. "Your testimony didn't do her any favors. On cross examination, Sloan Sutton was able to get on the record that Carol Simms was charged with a felony prostitution charge."

"That's another reason," Simon snarled, "why I should haven't been asked to testify."

Stephanie grimaced, "I think Lynne will do a better job next time in a similar situation."

He rolled his eyes. "What was the plea deal she made with Sutton?"

"Frank Rogers pled guilty to a simple promoting prostitution charge."

His eyes widened. "That's a misdemeanor with no jail time."

She pointed down at the file on the table. "Listen, Simon, I have a trial in twenty minutes. I don't have time to debate this matter."

Simon did not respond but whirled around and stormed out of the courtroom. He dreaded having to tell Carol how the trial played out. Simon decided to go back to his office and call to see if he could get an appointment to see her. It would be better to tell her in person.

Driving the short distance from downtown back to his office in the Oak Cliff Bank Building, his temperament turned livid. He felt an impending darkness he had not experienced since meeting Carol. His anger was directed not only at Frank Rogers but also Lynne Ellis, Sloan Sutton, and the whole turn of circumstances.

Simon almost forgot to deposit the check he had received in the mail the day before from Dallas County as a fee for one of his court appointed cases. Before he pulled in the bank's underground parking below, he decided to go through the drive-through.

Two uniformed security guards were posted on each side of the lanes. Each guard was armed with a holstered pistol and twelve gauge shot gun. Simon guessed that the bank went to these lengths to demonstrate to the public that there would be no bank robberies.

One of the guards, Harold Mapes, came over to Simon every time he pulled into the drive-through. He was an old car aficionado and loved Simon's 1966 Pontiac. Harold always engaged Simon in conversation while he was waiting in line for the next available teller.

Today, however, Simon was in no mood for small talk.

Harold tapped on the driver's side window and Simon rolled it down. "What's the matter, Simon? Everything all right?"

Simon sighed. "Yeah, I'm okay. Just a bad day."

Harold winked at him. "Whatever is wrong will soon get better."

Simon feigned a smile. "Thanks, Harold. Keep the bank safe."

Harold looked down at his twelve-gauge. "That's why I have ol' Betsy here."

The line moved, and Simon heaved a sigh of relief. "Take care, Harold."

Harold nodded and strolled back over to his normal post on the side of the driveway.

After Simon deposited his check, he parked his car in the underground parking lot and hurried up two flights of stairs to his office on the second floor, speculating that walking would be faster than waiting for the notorious slow elevator to arrive. Simon plopped down in his office chair, grabbed the phone receiver and dialed Carol's phone number. It rang nine times before Simon hung up.

Damn, I wished she was at home. I really want to tell her about Frank's case!

He tried dialing her number several more times throughout the long afternoon, but she still did not answer.

* * *

At 8:00 pm, Simon drove north on Harry Hines Boulevard. As he approached the Royal Lane intersection, his head jerked back and forth, checking both sides of the street.

A women dressed in a short black dress leaned against a stop sign, waving at every vehicle that passed. Simon pulled in the service station just north of the Royal Lane intersection and parked at the edge of the lot.

Two women stood in the shadows next to the building. He could not get a clear view, but wondered if they were the same two women he had encountered several weeks ago with Frank. After a few minutes, Simon eased the Pontiac back onto Harry Hines Boulevard and drove north.

Several cars were parked in front of a closed hardware store. Two men and a few women were congregated there. Simon could see well enough to determine that Carol was not among them. He decided to go back and made a u-turn.

As he approached the Royal Lane Intersection, the traffic light turned red. While idling, he sat watching the vehicles pass by in front of him going east and west on Royal Lane. His eyes widened when a black Camaro eased by heading west.

After a few seconds, the traffic cleared enough for Simon to make a right turn onto Royal Lane. The taillights of the Camaro came into view a few yards in front of him. It drove past several intersections before taking a right turn onto Reeder Road. Simon took a right on Reeder Road just in time to watch the Camaro pull into a parking lot on the right side.

He edged past where the Camaro turned. Over to the right was a dimly lit sign with the words 'Miramar Motel'. Simon wanted to turn in but at the last second drove on past.

If Frank sees my car, he's going to know it's me. I doubt if Carol is with him anyway.

Instead, Simon drove his Pontiac over to Carol's apartment complex. He eased into the parking space and walked down the uneven sidewalk toward her unit.

When he was a few yards away, he stopped in his tracks. No lights were on inside.

Carol's probably asleep or not at home. I hope the hell she's not out on Harry Hines Boulevard!

Chapter 31

At 5:00 p.m., Thursday afternoon, Simon tried Carol's number one last time. He had called her several times throughout the day. Simon slammed the receiver back down on the phone cradle, grabbed his briefcase, and headed down the stairs to the Oak Cliff Bank Tower parking garage.

The garage was almost deserted. Friday was a holiday and he suspected that most of the occupants of the building had gotten a head start on the weekend. As he approached his Pontiac, he thought he glimpsed the movement of a dark figure in the shadows near where he was parked. Simon pulled his keys out of his pants pocket and inserted one to unlock the driver's door.

A man's voice from the shadows said, "Well if it isn't Carol's guardian angel in the flesh."

Simon jerked around in the direction of the voice. A man dressed in blue jeans, a black shirt, and a blue sport coat emerged from the shadows. He brandished a pistol in his right hand.

Simon recognized him as soon as the smattering of overhead lights illuminated his face. A chill shot down his spine, but he was determined to maintain his composure.

"Frank Rogers. What brings you to a parking garage underneath the Oak Cliff Bank Tower?"

Frank took a step closer and was now only about five yards away. He sneered, "I'm here to take care of some business. Where does Carol live?"

Simon shrugged. "I don't know, Frank."

"You're lying."

Simon feigned a smile. "Frank, you're making a big mistake by pointing a pistol at me down here."

Frank wrinkled his forehead. "What are you talking about?"

"Oak Cliff Bank is right above us. Several security cameras are all over the place." Simon jerked his head to the left. "One right over there is pointed in our direction."

Frank shot a quick glance where Simon gestured. "You expect me to fall for that? The bank's closed."

Simon looked up. "The drive-through banking remains open until 6:00 p.m. and is manned by two guards armed with twelve-gauge shotguns. Another guard inside monitors the cameras and alerts all guards of any suspicious activity. I would think that seeing a man point a pistol in the parking garage would draw quite a bit of attention."

Rattled, Frank's eyes now darted around the garage. "You're bluffing."

Simon sighed. "I'm good friends with one of the guards. In fact, he wanted to purchase my car, just like you did, Frank, that night on Harry Hines

Boulevard. I suspect they'll be down here any second now."

Frank backed away. "You stay right where you are, you bastard, or I'll shoot."

Simon froze and waited. A few seconds later, a car's tires squealed as it careened in the direction of the exit.

He fumbled the keys, trying to unlock the Pontiac but was successful after a few attempts. Simon took several deep breaths to calm himself. His hands trembled.

Damn, that was close. How did he know where I parked?

He turned the key in the ignition and then drove at a slow pace through the parking garage toward the exit. As he drew near, sirens blared just outside. He eased out of the exit onto the driveway that led to Zang Boulevard.

Two police vehicles were parked just to the north, with their lights flashing. Simon parked in the driveway and exited the car. He hurried down the sidewalk in the direction of the police cars. An ambulance whizzed past him on Zang Boulevard and screeched to a halt a block down.

As Simon drew near the intersection of Zang Boulevard and Jefferson Boulevard, he spotted two cars, their fenders and bumpers mangled. Smoke rose above them.

He watched as several firefighters surrounded the two cars. One sprayed a fire extinguisher onto the engine of one of the vehicles. Two firefighters tried to pry the door open from a white pickup truck that was lodged into the side of a black car.

Simon walked up behind a police officer standing a few yards away from the crash scene. "What happened officer?"

The officer glanced over at him. "My guess is, that black Camaro ran the light, because that white pickup t-boned him."

Simon's eyes widened.

That's Frank's car! I wasn't provoked at all to have caused it. Was it just an accident?

He drew as close to the accident scene as the police would allow. At last, the firefighters were able to pry open the driver's side door to the pickup. They helped a man climb out.

His forehead was bloodied, but he was capable enough to walk, with the assistance of the firefighters. Two paramedics rushed over to the man and helped him to an ambulance.

The firefighters then turned their attention to the mangled Camaro. A third firefighter arrived with a jaws-of-life tool and began working on the door on the driver's side.

With the help of the other two, he cut through the exterior of the door and ripped off a huge chunk. Two of them pulled out a lifeless man's body and laid him gently on the sidewalk. The man's head was almost decapitated.

The small crowd of spectators gasped at the

sight. Simon recognized the clothing from his earlier encounter with Frank.

Paramedics from another ambulance rushed over. They kneeled around the blood-soaked, prone body, attempting to detect any pulse.

One of them shook his head. "He's dead."

* * *

As soon as he got home, Simon raced into his kitchen and grabbed the receiver off the wall phone. He dialed Carol's phone number as fast as he could. But the same as before, no one answered.

After letting out a big sigh, he wandered over to the refrigerator and grabbed a Coors Light and plopped down on the worn sofa in his den.

He wondered if Carol might have gone somewhere, since tomorrow was a holiday. It was possible she had family somewhere.

Thoughts kept flying through his head. One thing was certain, Frank didn't know her whereabouts.

Where was she? He realized he was becoming obsessed with finding her.

* * *

At 7:00 p.m., Simon backed the Pontiac out of his garage and drove the short distance to downtown Dallas. He had taken this route to Harry Hines Boulevard so many times, he could have done it with his eyes closed.

As he approached the Royal Lane intersection, the cars came to the usual slow crawl. His head jerked back and forth as he surveyed all the pedestrians on each side. A brunette woman wearing a blue jean miniskirt and sequined top waved at him. Simon slowed the Pontiac to get a closer look but shook his head and continued driving north.

He pulled in the service station just north of the Royal Lane intersection. He already had three quarters of a tank of gas but decided to fill his car anyway. It gave him the opportunity to look around without acting suspicious. When the pump chimed, he placed the nozzle back into the pump's holster.

Simon started his car and sat idling at the pump. He was about to shift into drive when he spotted a blond woman exiting the service station convenience store. Simon recognized her as the same blond Frank introduced to him a few weeks back at this same location. She was wearing the identical outfit as before.

He eased the car over to the parking space in the direction she was walking and rolled down his window. "Excuse me."

The woman stopped in her tracks and took a drag on a cigarette that she had lit when she exited the convenience store. She exhaled a cloud of smoke. "Hello, sweetie. Looking for some company?"

In a friendly demeanor, Simon smiled. "Do you remember me? I met you the other night when I was pumping gas."

She cocked her head to the left and wrinkled her forehead. "No. Did we have a date?"

Simon sighed. "Don't you remember? You, Frank, and another woman were standing on the side of the building. When you spotted me, Frank walked over to my car and engaged me in a conversation. After a few seconds, he called you over to meet me?"

The woman took a step back and shrugged. "I have no idea what you're talking about. I don't remember meeting you and I sure don't know anybody named Frank."

He frowned, "Frank Rogers. He drove a black Camaro."

She hissed, "Are you a cop?"

Simon shook his head. "No, I'm a lawyer. I'm trying to find a woman who's a client of mine. I was hoping you might be able to tell me if you've seen her. She worked for Frank. I suspect you do as well."

The woman pursed her lips. "You're crazy. I'm getting out of here." She charged down the sidewalk and disappeared behind the building.

She's obviously lying! But why? Does she know Frank died in a car crash this morning?

Simon pulled out of the service station and turned left and headed south on Harry Hines Boulevard. He joined the line of slow-moving vehicles, keeping a lookout for Carol. After Simon reached Mockingbird Lane, he decided to do a u-turn and drive up and down Harry Hines Boulevard one more time.

Before he reached the Royal Lane intersection, he

noticed a group of women clustered near a parked van. Simon pulled into the lot a parked a few yards away. Five women faced the opposite direction and appeared to be talking to the occupants of the van.

The woman in the middle of the group resembled Carol from the back. She had the same hair color and physique.

He rolled down his window and continued to stare at the women. It was too dark for him to be certain. The nearby streetlamp was not lit. The only lights indirectly illuminating the lot were cast from the vehicles passing by on Harry Hines Boulevard.

He couldn't restrain himself any longer, so he decided to satisfy his curiosity and shouted, "Carol."

All five women spun around and stared at him. The woman he had thought might be Carol did not even remotely resemble her in the face.

Simon rolled up his window, shifted into drive and spun out of the lot back onto Harry Hines Boulevard. He made a u-turn at the first available opportunity and headed back south. Simon considered driving by Carol's apartment but chose instead to go back to his home in Oak Cliff.

Since Frank didn't know where Carol lived, she's probably safe.

Chapter 32

Simon slept in on Friday. He pondered going into the office but opted to take the three-day holiday weekend off. After eating breakfast and reading the Dallas Morning News, Simon decided to go for a drive in his Pontiac. He was not certain of his destination until he pulled out of his driveway.

Simon chose to go to Lake Cliff Park on Zang Boulevard. The historic park was established in 1906, and at the time was dubbed "The Southwest's Greatest Playground".

Due to neglect by the City of Dallas, it had deteriorated over the years. Regardless, it still had beautiful green lawns and trees that surrounded a lake in the middle. Simon's parents used to bring him and his older brother here for picnics.

He parked his Pontiac along the side of the park. He exited his car and right away surveyed his surroundings.

Several families were already enjoying the amenities of the park. Some sat on blankets while others strolled across the grass.

Simon walked the entire perimeter of the park, and then he stopped at a bench just off the sidewalk and sat down.

A young man dressed in shorts and T-shirt and a Weimaraner dog came jogging by. Simon watched until they disappeared around the bend. Three young women wearing T-shirts and faded blue jeans ambled by in the other direction.

He guessed that they were close to the same age as Carol but were fortunate to live a different life. His thoughts drifted back to her.

Where is she right now? Is she with family or friends?

* * *

Simon felt invigorated after his walk. He drove over to Margaret B. Henderson Elementary School where he attended as a child. When he arrived, he pulled into the vacant teacher's parking lot and parked. Simon hadn't been back here since his parents moved away after he completed the six grade.

He exited his Pontiac and walked around to the front entrance to the school. The façade of the old brick school had not changed over the years.

Simon snickered as he recalled helping students cross the street a few yards away when he was finally made a school patrol in his last year there. There were some dark moments even back then, but most of his memories of this period of life were positive.

He pulled a compact disc out of his glove box and inserted it into the disc player mounted just under his dashboard. The sound of John Lennon singing the song *Imagine* reverberated through the interior of the Pontiac. Simon smiled as he drove the short distance back to his home.

I wonder how I 'll feel when Monday's business as usual?

Chapter 33

Simon arrived at his office at 8:00 a.m. Feeling refreshed from the long weekend, he debated whether to go down to the courthouse and try to pick up some court appointed cases or just work on the cases he already had.

Two motions he had filed a few weeks back were on the docket to be heard on Thursday and Friday. Simon opted to stay put and prepare for the two hearings.

He glanced at his watch; it was 10:30 am. Simon grabbed the receiver from the phone on his desk and dialed Carol's number. It rang ten times before he hung up.

I wonder if the D.A.'s office is aware that Frank Rogers died in a car crash?

He flipped through his card rolodex until he found the number for Stephanie Griggs and dialed it. The phone rang five times before it rolled to voicemail.

A man's recorded voice said, "You have reached 214-312-5951. I'm not available to take your call at the moment. At the sound of the tone, please leave your name, phone number and message and I'll return the call as soon as possible."

Simon said to the receiver, "Hello, this is Simon Steed. I'm trying to reach Stephanie Griggs. I have some information that might be of interest to her. Could you please have her call me at 214-948-7875. Thank you."

He surmised that she was probably trying a case in court.

I wonder why there's a man's voice on the answering machine?

At 3:00 pm., Simon grabbed the receiver from the phone's cradle and dialed Carol's number. Again, he let it ring ten times before hanging up. He considered if he should drive over to her apartment in northwest Dallas. Instead of taking the freeway, Simon chose a route through downtown Dallas and then north on Harry Hines Boulevard.

The scene at the Royal Lane intersection looked much different in the afternoon than at night. All the retail businesses were open and no person in sight resembled a sex worker. The vehicular traffic flowed at normal speeds going north and south of Harry Hines Boulevard.

Simon turned right onto Royal Lane and wound through a couple of residential neighborhoods before arriving at Carol's apartment complex. It seemed even more dilapidated than he remembered.

He pulled into a space and sat idling in the Pontiac. The door to her apartment was visible from his vantage point. Simon checked his watch for the time. It was 3:45 pm. He exited the Pontiac and ambled up the uneven sidewalk and paused in front of her door.

I hope she's home!

Simon knocked three times on the wooden door and waited. He stared, smiling at the peep hole in case she was peering out to see who knocked on her door.

After about a minute, the door cracked open just wide enough for the person inside to look out. The chain lock was still attached. A young dark-haired woman who appeared to be in her late twenties stared at Simon. Her expression revealed bewilderment, as she seemed puzzled to be face to face with him.

Simon said, "Good afternoon. Is Carol home?"

The woman's expression did not change.

A man's voice from inside said, "Who is it, Maria?"

She tucked her head back inside and said, "I don't know. It's some man."

A large man appeared at the door and stared at Simon. He sported a bald head and thick black beard, and was dressed in blue jeans. A stained white undershirt barely concealed his protruding stomach.

He furrowed his brows and then said through gritted teeth, "Is there something I can do for you?"

Simon feigned a smile. "I'm Carol's attorney. I was hoping to be able to speak with her. Is she home?"

The man frowned. "I don't know any Carol."

Simon wrinkled his forehead. "I know she lives here. I have been here several times before."

The man hissed, "I don't know what type of stunt

you're trying to pull. But, if I was you, I would get the hell of here while you still can."

Simon took a step back and held up his palms. "Take it easy. I'm not trying to agitate you."

The man sighed, "The only two people who live here are my girlfriend and me. Nobody named Carol lives here."

Simon said, "Okay, maybe she's moved. Will you at least tell me how long you have lived here?"

The man shrugged. "I don't know. Maybe two or three years."

Simon's eyes widened. He started to say something but stopped. "I'm sorry to have disturbed you."

The man slammed the door shut. Simon stood and stared at the closed door trying to process what had just happened.

Where the hell is Carol? Have these people done something to her? Should I call the police?

He got inside his Pontiac and stared at the door of the apartment. After a few minutes, he started the Pontiac and drove back to his home in Oak Cliff.

* * *

All the positive energy from the weekend had dissipated. Simon had no appetite but managed to down a small frozen dinner.

At 7:00 pm, he climbed into his Pontiac and headed over to Harry Hines Boulevard. The traffic was heavier than normal. When he arrived a few blocks south of the Royal Lane intersection, the cars were bumper to bumper and crawling along slowly going north. The southbound lanes were deserted.

Simon suspected that there must have been a traffic accident. An hour passed before he came within a few yards south of the Royal Lane intersection. His old Pontiac was smelling overheated.

About ten yards across the median ahead, several police cars were parked, preventing traffic from going south on Harry Hines Boulevard. Simon pulled over into the nearest parking lot and turned off the ignition. He knew all the signs when his old car was about to blow a gasket.

I might as well go see what's going on while my car cools down.

Simon walked up the sidewalk a few yards. When he got closer, he spotted a female body lying prone in one of the southbound lanes. He managed to cross the street to get a better look.

The woman's body lay face down. Her head was turned sideways facing his direction.

A sudden chill raced down his spine.

I hope that's not Carol!

He dashed down the sidewalk, attempting to get a closer look. One of the officers shifted to his left, which exposed the woman's face. Her face was badly bruised. She resembled Carol but her features were different.

Simon felt relieved but was saddened by the sight of this poor creature. He crossed Harry Hines

Boulevard to where his car was parked.

I have to get over this obsession with finding Carol!

Chapter 34

Simon spent a restless night, tossing and turning. He only got a few hours of sleep as he lay in bed most of the night reliving the day's events in his head.

After a cup of coffee, Simon drove straight to the George Allen Court House Building. He visited a couple of District Courts and managed to get appointed to three different cases.

At 9:30 a.m. Simon arrived at Judge Evers' courtroom. He opened the door and sneaked a peep inside, making sure no trial was already in progress. As usual attorneys were wandering around trying to hear plea deals from the prosecutor or filing motions on behalf of clients.

Simon did not recognize the prosecutor who stood in Stephanie's usual spot. The prosecutor appeared to be in his late thirties. He had a chestnut complexion and short black hair, and wore a white shirt, a red-and-blue striped tie, and a dark charcoal gray suit. Simon waited until he was alone before approaching him.

The man looked up when Simon drew near. "Can I help you?"

"Is Stephanie around?"

The man wrinkled his forehead. "Stephanie?"

Simon narrowed his eyes. "Stephanie Griggs, the chief prosecutor of this court."

The man cocked his head to the side. "That's not possible, because I'm John Holcombe, the chief prosecutor here."

Simon groaned. "What happened to Stephanie then? Did she get transferred?"

John shrugged. "Listen, I don't know any Stephanie Griggs in the D.A.'s office. Do you have a case in this court you want to discuss?"

Simon shook his head. "No, not now. But I do have some business I need to discuss with Stephanie. Is Lynne Ellis still part of your team?"

John's nostrils flared. "No, there's no one by that name on my team or in the D.A.'s office."

Simon felt his face flush with anger. "I saw her try a case against Frank Rogers in here just a few days ago."

John glanced over in the direction of the bailiff and motioned for him to approach. Both men watched as the bailiff ambled over to where they stood.

"What's up?" the bailiff said.

"How long have you been the bailiff in this court?" John said.

"Five years, why?"

John sighed. "Are any of the prosecutors who have ever worked here named either Stephanie Griggs or Lynne Ellis?"

The bailiff scratched his head. "No, I can't say I recall anyone by either of those names."

Simon's mouth dropped open. "But I know they're here."

Several attorneys now stood nearby, taking in the drama before them. Simon wheeled around and lurched toward the exit. He was trembling and his stomach gurgled with nausea.

What the hell's going on here?

Simon considered going home or to the park, or just driving around, but at last opted to go to his office.

Maybe I can sort through things when I get there.

Simon arrived at his office at 11:30 a.m. and plopped down into his office chair. He leaned back and closed his eyes.

What's happening to me? Am I hallucinating?

In the hallway just outside his office, people stirred, a daily occurrence around lunchtime. The door from the hallway that leads to his small reception area opened. Simon made the short trek across his office to the reception area.

A pale, thin woman in her early twenties, with expressive dark brown eyes and long straight brown hair, waited there, staring straight ahead with a blank expression. She was dressed in faded blue jeans and a white shirt.

Simon said, "May I help you?"

She cracked a slight smile. "Yes, you certainly may."

He was struck by her beauty and thought she looked vaguely familiar. "What is it I can do for you?"

"You don't recognize me do you, Simon?" Her smile faded.

Simon narrowed his eyes. "Have we met before?"

She ran a hand through her hair. "Does the name Thomas Hobbes ring a bell?"

He was even more perplexed. "Are you referring to Thomas Hobbes, the philosopher?"

The woman cackled. "Do you know any others?"

Simon wrinkled his forehead. "No, he's the only one. But why did you ask me that question?"

"I'm trying to help you to remember me."

He sighed. "I'm sorry. I don't recall having met you."

She sneered. "You were pretty damn infatuated with me in college."

Simon rubbed his head. "I knew you in college? But you're much younger than I am."

"I'll give you one more hint before I tell you why I'm here. Political Theory ring any bells?"

His eyes widened. "Monica? You can't be her. She would be my age now. Why are you doing this to me?"

Monica had an incredulous smile. "The first time I met you, I recognized your dark side and a special telepathic gift. After we met, I became your dominant personality. When you needed to be provoked, I was there for you. All was well, until you imagined you met Carol Simms."

Simon turned pale as beads of sweat broke out on

his forehead. "Stop, stop. I know I met Carol Simms. That was no imagination."

She snickered. "If that's the case, where is she now? Also, for that matter, where is Stephanie Griggs and Lynne Ellis? Finally, what about Frank Rogers?"

His whole upper torso trembled. "I saw Frank's body after he was killed in a car crash."

Monica nodded. "I'm sure you did, Simon."

Simon exhaled, trying to calm himself. "What do you want, Monica?"

She growled. "Never ever ignore Monica again!"

He opened his mouth to say something but could not articulate any words.

Monica turned around and exited the reception area and closed the door behind her. Simon sprinted across the room and swung open the door.

"Monica!" he shouted.

Several people stood outside, waiting for the elevator. They turned around and stared at him.

Simon threw his hands up. "Where did the woman go who just left my office?"

One of the men said, "We didn't see anybody exit your office."

Simon bent over at the waist. "She left just a second ago. You would've had to have seen her."

A woman rolled her eyes.

The man said, "Is this some kind of practical joke?"

Simon ran over to the door at the end of the hall which led to the stairs and hurried down two flights to the first floor. He threw open the door and scanned the area.

Monica was nowhere in sight.

Simon retraced his steps and trudged into his office and slumped down into his office chair. He stared at the ceiling.

I'll never ignore you again!

ACKNOWLEDGMENTS

This is my fifth novel with Treaty Oak Publishers. Cynthia Stone has provided exceptional guidance throughout the entire editing, cover design, and production of all my novels. I am very thankful to have her expertise throughout the whole process.

I would also like to thank Paulette Martsolf for diligently reading through various drafts of this book and offering helpful comments and edits.

ABOUT THE AUTHOR

After practicing law for many years, Jim decided to pursue his passion full time as a visual artist, film maker and author. He received the 2016 Merrimack Media Outstanding Writer Award for his second novel, *Punitive Damages*. *Arbitrary and Capricious* is the fourth novel in a series. *Choking on the Splinters* is the third novel in a series, a Global Book Bronze Award winner for Mystery and Suspense. *Surreal Absurdity*, also a Global Book Bronze Award winner is a sequel to his novel, *Aberrant Behavior*.

His artwork and art films have been recognized in numerous juried competitions, publications, and film festivals. He has exhibited his artwork in several group and solo exhibitions across North America and Europe.

Eighteen of Jim's films have been selected to various film festivals around the world. His art film, *The Soul of Vinyl, Abbey Road Side 2*, screened at the 2016 New York City Independent Film Festival. Jim's film, *The Case of the Deranged Sommelier* won Best Experimental Film in the 2016 Directors Circle of Shorts Film Festival and the 2017 Lion's Head Film Festival. His film, *Still Mad as Hell*, screened at the 2017 New York City Independent Film Festival. His film, *It's Gonna Disappear*, screened at the 2021 New York Flash Film Festival. His latest film, *Top Secret and Not So Confidential*, was selected as a Semi-Finalist in the 2023 San Jose Independent Film Festival.

Jim's education includes a Bachelor of Arts from The University of Texas at Austin, a Juris Doctor from Southern Methodist University in Dallas, and Level One Wine Sommelier Certification from the International Wine and Spirits Guild.

His website is www.jimlivelyart.com.